ELLEN FREMEDON,
VOLUNTEER

ELLEN FREMEDON, VOLUNTEER

by

Joan Givner

GROUNDWOOD BOOKS
HOUSE OF ANANSI PRESS
TORONTO BERKELEY

Groundwood Books / House of Anansi Press
110 Spadina Avenue, Suite 801, Toronto, Ontario M5V 2K4
Distributed in the USA by Publishers Group West
1700 Fourth Street, Berkeley, CA 94710

We acknowledge for their financial support of our publishing
program the Canada Council for the Arts, the Government of Canada
through the Book Publishing Industry Development Program (BPIDP)
and the Ontario Arts Council.

ONTARIO ARTS COUNCIL
CONSEIL DES ARTS DE L'ONTARIO

Library and Archives Canada Cataloguing in Publication
Givner, Joan.
Ellen Fremedon, volunteer / by Joan Givner.
ISBN-13: 978-0-88899-743-2 (bound).–
ISBN-10: 0-88899-743-4 (bound).–
ISBN-13: 978-0-88899-744-9 (pbk.) –
ISBN-10: 0-88899-744-2 (pbk.)
I.Title.
PS8563.I86E456 2007   jC813'.54   C2006-905649-8

Cover illustration by Rebecca Buchanan
Design by Michael Solomon
Printed in Canada

*To the memory of
Emily Givner
1966-2004*

CONTENTS

1
PEACEHAVEN

I WAS IN A very bad mood at the beginning of the summer, and meeting Mr. Martin didn't help. Actually, I'd been in a bad mood ever since my best friend, Jenny Brown, told me her dad was sending her to the Summer School for the Arts in Saskatchewan.

Jenny was really happy about it, and I felt terrible.

"This is not just crafts," she told me. "It's a real art school."

"That's great for you!" I said. "But my summer's ruined."

The day before she left, I sat on the top bunk of her bed, looking down as she packed a suitcase that lay open on the bottom bunk. Her art supplies were on her desk, and neat piles of clothes were stacked on the chairs. I didn't see how she was ever going to get there with all that stuff.

"What will I do for two whole months?" I said.

"Everyone's been asking about the paper," Jenny said.

Last summer we put out a newspaper, and the neighbors were expecting it again. Mrs. Banks and Mrs. Fenwick had already said they wanted a two-month subscription. But I couldn't do it without my business manager and art editor. There'd be no *Partridge Inquirer* this summer.

"Larry wants someone to read to the kids in the summer reading program at the library," Jenny said.

"I'm not going to waste my time reading to a lot of snot-nosed kids. Besides, the library never pays for anything. All they do is rake in your money for fines."

"Higg could use a babysitter," Jenny said. "He'd pay you."

"Yeah, right." Mr. Higginson was our favorite teacher, but I didn't feel like spending my summer holiday changing his kid's diapers.

"How about writing another book?" One summer I wrote a book about my family and how we tried to protect the village water system.

"I get enough of my family without writing about them," I said.

"Write about somebody else's family. You like doing book reports."

That was true. I did like reading history books and making notes on index cards. I did a report on a Russian princess called Anastasia who was murdered with her whole family when she was seventeen. For a long time, some people believed she'd escaped and lived out her life in another country. Women kept turning up and claiming they were Anastasia. Anyway, I got an A for the paper and even won a book certificate prize for it.

"Have you decided what to get with your book certificate?" Jenny said.

"Uh-uh." I was starting to think that school was more fun than holidays.

"Well, at least by the end of the summer you'll have tons of money saved up from your gardening jobs."

"Oh, great!"

I felt even worse the next day when I went with Jenny and her mother to the ferry to the mainland. Her mum and dad are divorced and her dad lives in Vancouver with his new wife. He was meeting her at the other side and taking her to the airport.

"Do you want me to drop you off at home or in

the village?" Jenny's mother said when we got back.

"Whatever."

So Anne dropped me in front of Mrs. A.'s Candy Kitchen, and I got a double-dip cone to cheer me up.

I was sitting outside eating it when Higg drove by in his truck. He stopped and backed up when he saw me.

"Hey, Ellen, I'm going out to Peacehaven with my singing group," he said. "Want to come along?"

"I hate singing in a group. I dropped out of the junior choir, you remember."

"You don't have to sing. You can just visit with the seniors. Jump in!"

It was more like an order than an invitation, and I jumped in before I remembered I wasn't in school and didn't have to do what he told me.

"What are you doing this summer?" he said.

"Nothing."

"Have you cashed in your book certificate yet?"

I wished people would stop asking me about the book certificate. The fact was I didn't have it anymore. I'd left it in the back pocket of my jeans when they went through the wash.

At Peacehaven there was a big room with a lot of ancient people in wheelchairs. Half of them were asleep.

A bunch of singers joined Higg around the piano and began to sing "My Favorite Things" and "Oh, What a Beautiful Morning." The old people who weren't asleep started nodding their heads and tapping their little feet in time to the music. A member of Higg's group sang "Spread a Little Sunshine" by herself, and the rest of the choir joined in with the chorus.

They sang a few more songs, and then it was time for a tea break. A young woman with KELLY embroidered on her uniform rolled in a trolley with cups of tea and plates of nasty-looking buns.

I was just wondering how soon we could leave when Kelly handed me a cup of tea and a plate with a bun on it. She told me to take it to Mr. Martin in his room up the hall.

"Third door on the right. Mind you don't spill!" she said.

It seemed like everybody was ordering me around.

I couldn't knock on the door because my hands were full, but it was slightly open so I just walked in.

It was a very bare room with brownish wallpaper that was turning yellow in places. Mr. Martin was sitting in a wheelchair by the window. He was wearing a grubby old sweater that had food stains all down the front, and worn-out bedroom slippers with his big toe sticking through a hole in one of them. He had no socks on.

"Who's that?" he said, turning in the direction of the door. His eyes were unfocussed and I could see he was blind.

"Ellen Fremedon," I said. "I've brought you some tea and a bun."

"That's not tea," he said. "It's pig swill. And that's not a bun. It's a rock. If you threw it at someone, you'd knock 'em out cold."

The tea was a nasty gray color because it had too much milk in it, and the bun did look like a rock.

"Would you like me to get you some fresh tea and something else to eat?" I said.

"You won't have much luck," he said. "They're trying to finish us off with the pig swill, if the noise doesn't do it first."

In the main room, I filled another cup from the urn, put a saucer on top to keep it warm, got a milk jug, and went back to Mr. Martin's room.

"I've got some fresh tea," I said. I wasn't sure what to do with it. I didn't know if a blind man could manage a cup and saucer.

"Well, don't just stand there," he said. "Give it to me." He stretched out his hand and found the handle of the cup, and I put the saucer in his lap.

"At least it's hot," he said.

"There was nothing to eat except the buns," I said, "but I've got a Kit Kat bar in my pocket."

He took the Kit Kat, but didn't say anything until the singing started up again.

"They call this place Peacehaven," he said, "but there's not much peace around here. They should call it Pandemonium. Wednesday's the worst. Are you visiting one of the old gals?"

"No. I came with my teacher. He's one of the singers."

"Think you could bring me some ginger snaps when you come next week?"

"I'm not coming next Wednesday, but I'll get the ginger snaps and give them to Mr. Higginson to bring."

He fished around in his pocket and gave me a five-dollar bill.

It was such an ugly room that I didn't know how anyone could stand to live in it. If Jenny saw it she'd probably get color samples from the paint store and swatches of different material and start talking about painting the walls and making curtains to match. Then I figured that it didn't really matter if you were blind.

After a while the music stopped, and I was worried that Higg might leave without me, and I'd have to walk all the way home. So I said goodbye, picked up the cup and plate and left.

Higg was chatting with the people in wheelchairs, and it was another half hour before he was ready to leave.

"Mr. Martin's very rude and grumpy," I said to Higg.

"You'd be grumpy, too, if you were blind, stuck in a wheelchair and never got any visitors," Higg said.

"Mum's in a wheelchair and she gets grumpy, but she's grateful when you get things for her, and she isn't rude to people she's only just met."

"She has a family to keep her company."

"Well, I don't like him. He never says please or thanks."

"You have to make allowances. Just think how you'd feel if your grandmother was in his shoes."

I didn't like thinking of Mum or Gran ending up in a place like Peacehaven where nobody bothered to change your clothes when you spilled on them, or get you new slippers when the old ones wore out. Mum always looked nice, and if she spilled on her blouse when her hands shook while she was eating, someone got her a clean one. I knew because I was usually the one who had to do the wash.

"He wants you to take him some ginger snaps next week," I said. "He gave me five dollars. Here."

"I'm not going out there next week. I have to take Thumper to Victoria for some tests," Higg said. "You get them and drop them off. It'll only take you fifteen minutes to ride out on your bike."

That made me so mad I wished I had a rock bun to throw and knock someone out cold.

The only good thing that happened all day was that I ran into Pat from the bookstore and she told me she had a load of new books in.

"You should come and take a look, because you haven't used your gift certificate yet."

"I don't have it anymore. I left it in my jeans pocket, and it went through the wash and got ruined."

"That doesn't matter," she said. "We have a record of it."

So I went to the bookstore and browsed through the new books. I didn't pick one out, though. I'd have plenty of time on my hands for the next two months, so I thought I might as well drag out the browsing as long as I could.

2
AT THE LIBRARY

I MET DIMSIE FAIRCHILD just before I went back to Peacehaven to take Mr. Martin the cookies and a bunch of flowers. It was Mum's idea to take the flowers.

"Ellen, are you going to put in a load of washing?" she said.

It seemed that every single time I wanted to go out, Mum had a chore for me to do. We didn't have much help around the house since Mrs. T., our last housekeeper, left. Dad kept running ads in the paper, but every time a person showed up about the job, the house was in a worse mess than usual. The last time someone came the living room was not only a mess, it was also stinking from rotten seaweed. The twins had brought in long strands of kelp with bulbs on the end from the beach. They'd been wrapping it around their arms and pretending to take their blood pressure.

They'd bought a medical dictionary for a dollar off the rack of old books outside the library, and now all they talked about was illness and disease, as if we didn't have enough of that in our house. They spent their allowance on medical supplies at the drugstore, so there were always Band-aids and Q-tips scattered all over the floor.

Anyway, no one wanted to work for a family with a stinky house, an invalid mother and three kids. So Dad and I ended up doing a lot of extra jobs as well as the cooking. I usually got stuck doing the laundry.

"I'll put the wash in later," I said. "I have to go out to Peacehaven to take an old man some cookies."

"That's kind of you," Mum said. "Why don't you take him some flowers as well?"

"He can't see flowers," I said. "He's blind."

"Well, he can smell them," Mum said. "Pick ones that have a strong scent."

So I ended up picking a bunch of pinks and stocks and sweetpeas and putting them in the basket on my handlebars with the cookies and some library books I had to return. I also picked up a raspberry smoothie on the way.

When I took the books into the library, Larry told me I had a humongous fine.

"There's no way I can owe over three dollars," I said.

"The books are two weeks overdue," Larry said.

"But Monday was a holiday."

"I've taken that into account."

"Don't you make an exception when somebody's sick?"

"No, I do not."

"What if I bring a note from my doctor saying I've had a life-threatening illness?"

"Ellen, you have not had a life-threatening illness."

"It's a hypothetical question, Larry."

"Well, I don't have time for hypothetical questions. I'm up to my ears in work."

"You know, Larry, you're a classic case for a heart attack." I was starting to sound like the twins.

"Is that so? Well, if all library users were like you, I'd have had one long ago."

Just then Miss Jane Green, the head librarian, came bustling out of her office.

"Now what's going on here?" she said.

"Ellen's giving me a hard time about her fine."

"I was just wondering if could pay it in instalments," I said. "I haven't been doing much gardening and I've had a lot of expenses lately. I'm a bit short of money."

"That seems reasonable enough," Miss Green said.

"I could manage a dollar today, and the rest later," I said. I pulled a handful of change out of my pocket and started counting out nickels and dimes.

"And how many times do I have to tell you that eating and drinking are not allowed in the library?" Larry said.

"I'm not eating and drinking in the library," I said. "I'm just carrying a Styrofoam cup with a lid on it."

"Well, there are other people needing attention here," he said.

There was a girl with long blonde hair standing behind me.

"I'm not in a hurry," she said.

Anyway, I picked up my Styrofoam cup and stomped out.

"Ellen is getting more impossible all the time," I heard Larry say.

"I guess she's at loose ends without Jenny," Miss Green said.

I was sitting on the brick wall just outside the

library finishing my drink, when the girl with the long blonde hair came out and walked up to me.

"I can lend you some money," she said.

When we got to know each other better she told me she felt stupid as soon as she said it, but it was the only way she could think of to start a conversation.

"That's okay," I said. "I actually have four dollars. It's just a matter of principle. Larry runs that place like it's the army, all rules and regulations. It's getting to be the same way all over the village. Don't touch the grapes! Don't squeeze the mangoes! Don't read the magazines unless you want to buy them! What is this, a prison camp? Are you the girl that's staying with Mrs. Broster?"

Rumors had been flying around the village that a young girl was visiting Mrs. Broster. We were all surprised because nobody even knew she had a family.

Ever since she moved to Partridge Cove, Mrs. Broster had lived alone in a big dark house called The Meads. It was a very creepy house. Even the garden was creepy. It was full of pine trees and laurels and rhododendrons, with hardly any flowers except a few bluebells and wild cyclamen under the bushes in spring. Ivy and convolvulus and broom had taken over. I went over there once and offered to do some weeding but Mrs. Broster said it was okay the way it was. Which was fine with me. You wouldn't know where to start with a mess like that.

There was a long twisty driveway and the trees met overhead, so it looked like a long dark tunnel. Most of the windows were shuttered and there was a weathervane on the roof that creaked in the wind. The kids would never go to the door on Hallowe'en or when there was a bottle drive at school.

I don't believe in ghosts myself. But I wouldn't want to stay there for one night, let alone the whole summer.

"Mrs. Broster's my grandmother," the girl said. "I'm Dimsie Fairchild and I feel like I'm in prison, too."

Just then Mrs. Banks came by with an armful of large-print books.

"Has Jenny left already?" she said.

"She left yesterday," I said.

"Then I'm glad I ran into you. You must have plenty of free time and my horsetails are getting completely out of hand. Can you come over and do something about them?"

"Sure."

"Well, don't leave it too long," she said, and went into the library.

"How many horses does she have and what's wrong with their tails?" Dimsie said.

"Horsetails are a plant," I said. "They're a kind of weed. They've been around since the time of the dinosaurs and so they're tough to get rid of."

"Who's Jenny?"

"My best friend. She went away for the summer. Why do you feel as if you're in prison?"

"I'm from Toronto, and I'm used to a big city, where you can just get on the subway and go downtown or wherever you want. This is the middle of nowhere and there's nothing to do."

"Well, why did you come out here, then?"

"They made me."

"Who did?"

"My other grandmother and my dad. He's doing a course at a university in Boston this summer, and she's gone over to Scotland."

"What about your mum?"

"I don't have a mum."

"Everybody has a mum!"

"Don't be stupid! A lot of people only have a single parent. I just have a dad."

"What would you be doing if you were in Toronto now?"

"Tons of things. Playing the piano. I was accepted into this summer music school that's very hard to get into and very expensive. Only one third of the people who apply are picked. I don't know anybody here except my grandmother, and she's shut up in her study writing letters and reading all day long. So I'm bored out of my skull. What do you do to kill time?"

"Various jobs," I said.

"What kind of jobs?"

"Mainly gardening for people. But just now I'm going out to Peacehaven."

"What's Peacehaven?"

"It's a home for seniors."

"You mean old people?" Dimsie said. "Do you have to feed them and clean them up?"

"No. I'm taking some stuff to an old man," I said. "Cookies and a bunch of flowers. Yoicks! If I don't get out there right away the flowers'll be dead."

I finished my drink in a gulp, tossed the cup into the garbage container, jumped on my bike and rode off.

"See you!" I said.

I was sorry for that girl with no mother, who had to live at the The Meads with a scary grandmother. But I didn't like her. She called me stupid, even though she asked those really dumb questions about horsetails. Even the twins knew what they were. She was snobby and rude, too. I didn't appreciate her saying that Partridge Cove was in the middle of nowhere, and what a big deal Toronto was. Jenny got into a summer school for the arts but she didn't go around bragging about it.

Thinking about Jenny made me remember how much I was missing her, so I thought I'd write her a letter. I'd tell her all about the weird kid I'd met outside the library, and all the stupid things she'd said.

She even had a stupid name.

3
MR. MARTIN

THIS TIME MR. MARTIN had a different sweater on but it was stained like the other one, and his toe was still sticking out of his slipper.

When I went in, he called out, "Who's there?" Then he said, "What's that smell?"

"It's me, Ellen Fremedon. I brought you some flowers. I'll get something to put them in."

I went to find Kelly. She was in the staff kitchen drinking a cup of coffee and flipping through an old movie magazine from the pile that visitors left behind. Somebody must have been bored to death because they'd drawn glasses on the faces of all the movie stars.

"I brought Mr. Martin some cookies and flowers and I need a vase," I said.

"Oh, Ellen, Mr. Martin isn't allowed to have cookies," Kelly said. "He's diabetic and anything sweet could make him ill."

"But he told me to get them."

"Well, he's very manipulative. Don't do everything he tells you. Just distract him and he'll soon forget what he asked for. Don't give him the cookies."

She couldn't find a vase, so she gave me an old mayonnaise jar.

"Say, Ellen," she said as she handed it to me. "You know that good-looking teacher of yours?"

"Mr. Higginson?" I said. "Some of the kids call him The Hulk, but he's nice."

"Is he married?"

"Yes, and he's got a kid."

"Shoot," Kelly said. "All the good-looking guys around this place are married. I don't think I'll ever meet Mr. Right." And she went back to her magazine.

Luckily, Mr. Martin seemed to have forgotten about the cookies. He was sniffing the flowers.

"Tell me what these are," he said.

"There's stocks, sweetpeas, pinks and a rose."

"Tell me what color they are," he said. So I described all the colors the best I could.

After a while, he pulled a piece of paper out of his pocket and unfolded it.

"Think you could read this letter?" he said. "You can read, can't you?"

"Of course I can."

He told me it was from his son who was an RCMP officer and lived in Nunavut.

"Where's Nunavut?" I said.

"It's up in the Arctic. It's where the Inuit live. Nunavut means 'Our Land.' Don't they teach you kids any geography?"

"We do social studies," I said, "but we haven't taken the Arctic yet."

"Well, you are ignorant."

That was the second time in one morning that someone had called me stupid, and it made me so mad I nearly threw the letter in his lap and walked out.

"Go on, read it," he said. "You might learn something."

I started reading the letter very fast so I could get it over with and get out of there, but it was actually interesting. It was all about the northern lights in the sky:

Dear Dad,
Many thanks for your last letter and the package of tea. We drink a lot of it up here at this time of year.

For the past two days we've had amazing displays of lights. Last Sunday there was a broad ribbon of white in the sky. As I looked at it, it kept moving, splintering apart and then reforming, turning from white to light green to a glowing emerald color. As I was walking home yesterday, I saw the whole sky fill up again with white ribbons that swirled about and turned from white to green.

On some nights, the northern lights make a loud cracking sound like somebody cracking a whip. I hope that one of these days you'll be able to fly up here and see them for yourself.

Hope your legs aren't bothering you too much.

Yours,
Rupert

I wondered if he'd forgotten his dad was blind and in a wheelchair, or if he was just saying that to cheer him up.

"I never wrote back," Mr. Martin said when I finished.

"Why not?" I realized it was a stupid question as soon as I said it.

"I could help you write a letter," I said to make up for the silly question.

"You could," he said, "but I don't have anything to write with." So I went and asked Kelly for paper and a pen.

"What do you want to say?" I said.

"Tell him I'm having a great time at Peacehaven."

"But you aren't."

"No," he said. "But that's the sort of stuff you put in a letter. It's like putting 'having a wonderful time' when you write a postcard."

"But people are having a wonderful time when they write postcards because they're usually on holiday."

"When was the last time you went on holiday?" he said.

"We never go anywhere because my mum's got M.S. and she can't travel."

"Well, let me tell you something, Ellen," he said. "People generally have a lousy time on holiday. Their luggage goes missing, the weather's rotten, they pick up bugs, and they get upset stomachs. If they're on a cruise ship, they all come down with some virus. But nobody writes a postcard saying, 'Weather lousy. Luggage lost. Got diarrhea. Wish I'd stayed home.'"

"If holidays are so bad, why does everybody say how great they are?"

"They don't want their friends to know they've made damn fools of themselves, traipsing all over creation and spending a lot of money just to come down with a bug. And they don't want people feeling sorry for them. It's the same reason sick people say, 'Fine thanks' when somebody says, 'How are you?' Anyway, nobody wants to hear about your arthritis and heart attacks and high blood pressure."

"My brothers do. Illness is all they want to talk about."

"Well, you should bring them out here. They'd have a field day."

"So you're saying everybody tells lies all the time?"

"If everybody told the truth," he said, "we'd all go nuts."

"No, we wouldn't. I wouldn't feel bad if I knew people had a rotten time on their holidays. I feel bad because everyone except me gets to go places."

"You must be a nasty little girl then," he said.

"I'm not nasty and I'm not a little girl."

"Got a temper, too, haven't you?"

I was about to say I'd had it up to here with his insults when Kelly popped her head around the door and said it was nearly time for lunch. The morning had gone so fast I realized I was going to be late for my own lunch.

"We'd better finish this letter another time," Mr. Martin said. "See you tomorrow."

"Kelly, I don't want to come back tomorrow," I said as we walked down the corridor.

"Don't worry, if you don't want to," Kelly said. "He'll soon forget about it."

"Did your friend like the flowers?" Mum asked me at lunch.

"He's not my friend," I said. "I guess he liked the flowers but they didn't have anything to put them in. I had to stick them in a crummy old mayonnaise jar. And he couldn't eat the cookies because he's diabetic."

"We have extra vases in the garden shed," Mum said. "Why don't you take one of those?"

"They have cookies without sugar at the store," Toby said. "You should have got them."

"Mr. Weeks is a diabetic and he gets a lot of special stuff," Tim said. "There's a special powder he puts in his coffee instead of sugar. You should get some of that, too."

I hadn't planned to go back to Peacehaven, but I remembered I hadn't handed over the change I got when I bought Mr. Martin's cookies. I thought I might buy some diabetic cookies with it the next day. I'd take the cookies and a vase out to Peacehaven and finish Mr. Martin's letter. Then that would be the last time I'd go out there.

4
FIRST MEETING

I FORGOT ALL ABOUT Dimsie Fairchild until later that day. I'd gone over to help Mrs. Banks with her horsetails.

Everybody has a different idea about how to get rid of them. If you pull them up, it stimulates the root system and they get even worse. Some people put white vinegar on them, but Mrs. Banks said she didn't want her garden smelling like a fish and chip shop. So I cut them off near the root and put them on the compost heap. They make excellent compost because they're full of nutrients.

It was pretty hard work, but I made eight dollars.

On the way home I took a short cut across a

bunch of back gardens. When I crossed the bottom of Mrs. Broster's garden, I looked up at the house.

It was as dark and gloomy as ever, with most of the windows shuttered, but there was a square of light in the window of one of the downstairs rooms. And in that square of light I saw Dimsie Fairchild. She was sitting at a desk writing.

I don't know why, but I walked up the garden and tapped on the window.

Dimsie jumped. Then she saw it was me and pushed open the window.

"Sorry I rushed off this afternoon," I said. "I was in a hurry and I was in a bad mood."

"That's okay. I was in a bad mood, too."

"What are you doing?"

"Answering a letter from my friend Uma in Toronto."

"She sent you a letter already?"

"No. She gave me this letter when she came with my dad to see me off at the airport." She handed me the letter from her friend:

Only dear places Dim sum hi! By morning the dark time for you to read about this if you ever will now be far in on the fast airplane. I find hope for you who are always having evermore a food good eating flight. The horse stamps heavily are breathing so hard that donkey you rode can bite write through very sleeve often stables and lessons tell lonely me riding every stampede single wild thing roaring you bronco are calf-roping doing. We kangaroo may zoo as park well often practice zip codes stamps while postage we know write well. I'll do write good and elephant tell trunk you tusks how hide I clump get circus on wheels at seals the fate job. I'll ringmaster keep acrobats a dancing diary tightrope too tent and candy we eat can cheerfully swap clowns when somersaults you turn come sliding back. Now monkeys it's performing your hat turn about to right write left.

"I can't understand a word of it," I said.

"It's in a code we use. We started it in second grade when we were playing spies. We invented codes so we could send secret messages. Then we got email and we started using codes again. Uma has a lot of brothers and she didn't want them reading our messages."

"Neat!" I said. "Is it hard?"

"Not once you have the key. You don't read all the words. Just certain ones."

"How do you know which ones?"

"It goes by number. That's the key."

"Do you always use the same number?"

"No, that would make it too easy. You have to keep changing the numbers. You take the day of the week when you're writing the letter, subtract 2, and that's the key. Monday is Day One.

The date on the top of the letter was July 4, and that was a Thursday. So I did some quick arithmetic and managed to decode Uma's letter.

"That's neat," I said. "I should use a code like that because my brothers are always getting into my stuff."

Then she handed me her letter to her friend. She said they often use the same code for the reply. She was just working on the letter and she'd only got half of it in code.

Oh dear U can't MA greetings imagine! Monster it tyrannosaurus is dinosaur even carnivorous worse Jurassic than film I park thought. Let your alphabet letters which are on the outside only when things grow that policemen can not stop over me who from coming going far up on the garden wall even so please go please leave please don't write front back for as too soon for as ever you will get for this. It's   really   weird   here.

Most   of   the   rooms   in   the
house   are   closed   off   and   the
doors   locked.   There's   no   TV   or
radio.   Nan   won't   let   me   use
her   computer   and   she   doesn't
even   like   me   using   the   phone.
She   spends   all   her   time   working
in   her   office.   She   says   she's
working   on   family   history.   She
hardly   talks   to   me   most   of   the
time.   She   doesn't   even   notice   I'm
here.

"That's terrible," I said after I read it. "Why did she even invite you out here?"

"She didn't. It was my dad. He said it was time she took an interest in me. I don't think she wanted me to come. She's never had anything to do with us."

She looked as if she was about to start crying.

"Why don't you come out?" I said.

"I can't. She's gone to bed and the place is all locked up for the night."

"So climb out the window."

I got a plant pot for her to step on and helped her out and we walked down the garden and sat leaning against a log in the long grass and talked.

"Are your parents divorced?" I said.

"No. My mother died after I was born."

"How did she die?"

"I think it was in a car accident. I'm not sure."

"You're not sure? Aren't you curious?"

"Well, nobody talks about her."

"Nobody talks about her?"

"No. Do you think that's weird?"

"Maybe not," I said. "I actually have two mothers because I was adopted, but I don't know anything about the mother who put me up for adoption. I don't think about her all that much. Jenny thinks that's funny because I'm generally very nosy."

Dimsie didn't say anything so maybe she thought I was nosy, too. Except she didn't seem to mind telling me about herself.

She hated being in Partridge Cove. She said her grandmother scared her sometimes. She'd stare at her in a weird way as if she wondered why she was there. The whole place creeped her out. There was no TV and she wouldn't let Dimsie use her computer.

"My dad never lets us use his computer," I said.

Dimsie said she had her own computer and her own TV in her room in Toronto. She played video games and messaged her friends and she watched TV all the time. She and Uma had planned to take tennis lessons together.

But the thing she missed most was her piano. She'd been practicing like crazy all year so that she could get into this special program at the conservatory of music where all the best teachers were. But she needed to audition in September, and if she didn't practice all summer she wouldn't be ready.

"Granny Broster doesn't even like hearing music in the house," she said. "She's just like my dad. He didn't even want to get me a piano but my other grandmother wanted one. She even pays for my lessons. I don't know how I'm going to get through the summer."

She'd made a calendar for the next two months, and every day she crossed off one of the squares.

I said I felt the same way about not having Jenny around, and I told her about the things we usually did during the summer. I told her about the old potting shed at the bottom of our garden that my parents had fixed up and painted so I could have a place of my own and some privacy away from the twins. Jenny called it Somecot, which is short for Something Cottage, and we spent a lot of time there.

Dimsie said she'd love to see it so I told her I'd come and get her at the same time the next day and we could go to Somecot and make smoothies.

That seemed to cheer her up a bit, and she asked me to come over as soon as I could the next evening. Then we walked up the garden and I helped her climb back through her window.

I liked her better than I did the first time, but I still thought she was pretty spoiled. I felt kind of sorry for her because she sure had a weird family, but then I guess most families are a bit weird.

It was too late to write Jenny when I got home, so I put it off until the next day.

5
THE MOUSE HOUSE

MUM DOESN'T GET OUT much, and she likes to hear what I do during the day, so I told her I'd met a girl from Toronto who has no mother and a creepy grandmother who never leaves the house.

"I hope you didn't quiz her about her family," Mum said. "It could be a very painful subject."

"Ellen always sticks her nose into other people's business. She's nosy just like the Elephant's Child," Tim said. Dad was reading the twins the *Just So Stories* at night.

I asked Mum what she knew about Mrs. Broster.

"I don't think anybody knows much about her," Mum said. "Perhaps Gran does. I believe their paths crossed in the city before she bought The Meads."

"Sean Floyd says she's a witch," Toby said.

"Sean Floyd watches too much TV and talks utter nonsense," Dad said.

"He didn't see it on TV. He saw it on the internet," Tim said.

"Dimsie says her grandmother's house is creepy, though," I said. "A lot of the rooms are locked up."

"Well, it's a huge house," Mum said. "She probably shuts parts of it up to save on heating bills and cleaning. I must say we all thought it odd that a person living alone should buy such a big place."

"Why do you think she did?"

"Who knows? Perhaps she has valuable furniture or artifacts that she wanted to store."

"Maybe she has kleptomania," Tim said.

"Or agoraphobia," Toby said.

"Too bad Ellen doesn't know anything about diseases."

"I just hope she doesn't pick up a hanta virus or something from going over there. She could start an epidemic."

"What's going to start an epidemic around here is you two looking into people's mouths with popsicle sticks that have been all over the floor," I said.

"They're not popsicle sticks. They're tongue depressors."

"All the same," Mum said, "that house can't be a very comfortable place for your friend. Tell Dimsie she's welcome to come over here. Why don't you invite her for lunch on Sunday?"

"When she's been over here for a few hours, she'll probably be thrilled to get back to a quiet place," Dad said.

I decided I'd invite Dimsie over when I saw her that evening. But first I had to go out to Peacehaven to drop off the diabetic cookies and finish Mr. Martin's letter to his son. I'd also found an old pair of Dad's bedroom slippers. They were a little beat up, but at least they didn't have holes in them, and I was sure they'd fit.

But when I got there, Mr. Martin's room was empty.

"They've taken him to the hospital for some tests," Kelly said. "Go in and talk to Miss Gwillam instead. She likes a bit of company. Take her these clean towels."

Before I could say anything, she'd given me an armful of towels and pointed me towards the door at the end of the corridor. I'd seen this door before and wondered what it was. It had a knocker like the front door of a house, and there was a bell pull with the words PLEZ KNOCK beside it.

Miss Gwillam must have heard my footsteps coming down the hall and stopping at the door because she called out, "Enter!" while I was trying to decide whether to knock or ring.

When I went in, I found myself in a very large room with a view of the lake. A woman wearing a straw hat and writing on a pad of notepaper was sitting beside a huge doll's house.

She smiled at me.

"What a great doll's house!" I said.

"It isn't a doll's house," Miss Gwillam said. "It's a mouse house. Come and look."

When I was close up I could see stuffed mice dressed in doll's clothes sitting on chairs in the different rooms. It was a beautiful house with a peaked roof, three bedrooms upstairs and a dining room, sitting room and kitchen downstairs. The kitchen had a stove with a saucepan on it, and there were tiny cups and saucers on the tables. There was even a miniature Christmas tree in a corner of the living room.

"Why do they all have bandages on their tails?" I said.

"If you sit down, I'll tell you all about them," Miss Gwillam said. So I sat on the window seat.

"Mousefield Park is a large house in the country. It's the home of a family of field mice. There are five sisters and their names are Jessie, Jemima, Japonica, Josephine and Jasmine."

Then she dropped her voice and leaned close to me. She smelled like a bed of lavender.

"Soon after Jasmine was born, Mr. and Mrs. Mousefield had a nasty accident involving a cat." Then she went on in a normal voice.

"Jessie, Jemima, Japonica and Josephine felt very sorry for their little sister who never knew her parents, and they tended to spoil her. Unfortunately, she became a rather selfish little mouse who didn't know how to share or think of others.

"At Christmas time, there were heaps of presents under the Mousefields' Christmas tree. As they opened their presents, Jessie, Jemima, Japonica and Josephine passed around the boxes of cheese and bacon bits for the others to nibble. But Jasmine just set hers aside to eat later, all by herself. What do you think of that?"

"It's just the kind of thing my brothers would do," I said. Miss Gwillam ignored me and went on with her story.

"When all the presents were opened, one last present remained under the tree. It was beautifully wrapped and it had Jasmine's name on it. There

was a card that read FROM A SECRET FRIEND.
Do you know who it was from?"

"No."

"It was from Jasmine to herself. She bought it
because she was afraid she might not get everything her heart desired."

Just then a loud meow outside the door made
me jump.

"What was that?" I said.

"Oh, it's just Mr. Martin," she said. "He does it to
annoy. Pay no attention."

"I brought some things for his tea," I said. "I'd
better go and give them to him."

"Very well," Miss Gwillam said, "but if you come
back another day, I'll finish the story about how
Jasmine Mousefield learned to think of others."

"Thank you," I said. I felt like I was in nursery
school again.

"And I wonder if you could help me with something," she said. I looked at the writing pad on her
lap. I hoped she wasn't going to ask me to help with
a letter, since I already had my hands full with Mr.
Martin.

"It depends," I said.

"Do you think you could pick up some white
cotton tape? Jessie-Jemima-Japonica-Josephine-
and-Jasmine would be so grateful."

"Is it for the bandages?" I said.

"Oh, they're not bandages," Miss Gwillam said. "They're for curling their tails. Field mice are very vain about their beautiful long tails."

She reached for her purse and gave me a five-dollar bill.

"The tape won't be more than three dollars," she said. "You can keep the change."

"Wow. Thanks."

"Will it be hard to think of something to spend it on?"

"No," I said. "I'm always getting library fines because I forget to take my books back on time."

"So you've been visiting Josephine Gwillam, have you?" Mr. Martin said, after he got his tea. "She's ga-ga, you know."

"That's a very nice mouse house she has," I said.

"She plays with it all day," he said. "You don't think that's wacko?"

She may be ga-ga but at least she's polite, I thought.

"I've brought you some special cookies," I said, "and a pair of slippers that don't have holes in them," I bent down and put them on his feet.

"I kinda like the one with holes in them," he said. "They let my toes breathe and keep them cool in this hot weather. Let's try those cookies."

I gave him a cookie and said we should finish his letter. I read the sentence we'd written the day before.

"What else do you want to tell him?" I said.

"Tell him I went to the hospital and they stuck needles in me and took pictures of my insides and checked my plumbing, and said I should be well enough to fly up and see him pretty soon."

It didn't look to me like he'd be flying anywhere soon, but I thought if I argued about it we'd never get the letter finished, so I just put down what he said in my own words.

"Anything else?" I said.

But Mr. Martin was falling asleep, so I put the letter away again and said I'd come back tomorrow. I figured I had to come back anyway with Miss Gwillam's tape.

When I got to the village, I went straight to the Clothes Loft. Mrs. Floyd was behind the counter.

"Thin white tape," she said. "What d'you want it for?"

"It's for one of the seniors at Peacehaven."

"And what would she be needing it for?"

"She has some mice," I said. "She uses it to curl their tails."

"Mice?" Mrs. Floyd said. "They let them keep mice?"

"Oh, no," I said quickly. "These are just toy mice."

"Good grief!" Mrs. Floyd said. "It must be a mad house out there. Those poor nurses deserve every penny they earn."

"Did Mr. Martin enjoy his cookies?" Mum asked when I got home.

"Not really," I said. "He'd been having tests at the hospital, and he was too tired to eat much. I visited a lady who has a doll's house full of toy mice in her room. Do you think that's crazy? She talks about the mice as if they're real people."

"Maybe she's lonely," Mum said, "and the doll's house reminds her of a happy time in her child-hood."

"That's sad," I said.

I decided I'd take her some flowers the next day. She'd probably be a lot more grateful than Mr. Martin.

6
DIMSIE'S ROOM

I GOT MY FIRST postcard from Jenny that day. She always makes her own by cutting one of her drawings to fit an index card and sticking it on with double-sided tape. It was a watercolor painting of a grain elevator, and even the stamp was a painting of a grain elevator. When Jenny mails anything she spends a long time at the post office picking out the prettiest stamps.

This is what she wrote on the back:

Dear Ellen,
I really like it here. Today we did gesture drawings. These are drawings that are very abstract. The idea is just to feel the motions of moving things or still things. After lunch we

saw a film about Matisse. When he was in
hospital and could hardly move he didn't stop
drawing. He took a long bamboo pole and got
charcoal on the end of it. He then reached the
pole up to the ceiling and drew on the ceiling
of the hospital. Write and tell me everything
you are doing.

Love Jenny

"Ask Jenny what was wrong with that man who couldn't sit up in bed," Toby said at supper.

"That was a private postcard and you had no business reading it," I said.

"I bet he got paralysis from being bitten by a spider or a snake," Tim said.

"You'd need a pretty long pole to draw on your bedroom ceiling," Toby said.

I knew what was going through his mind. Dad had forbidden the twins to draw on their walls, but he hadn't said anything about the ceiling.

In the middle of supper, the storm broke. There was a terrific crack of thunder and then lightning, and it started to pour. I was mad because I'd been looking forward to going over to Dimsie's to ask her for Sunday lunch and seeing her cheer up. I'd planned to get the dishes done fast and then rush over to her house. She'd climb out of the window and we'd sit talking on the steps of Somecot until it got dark.

Now the storm had ruined everything.

I took my time with the dishes and then went to my room. I'd decided to write Jenny and tell her to use the code so the twins couldn't read her post-cards. But I kept thinking how disappointed Dimsie would be when I didn't turn up, so I decided to go anyway. The thunder and lightning had stopped but it was still raining hard.

Dimsie was sitting at her desk by the window, but she wasn't writing. When I got closer I could see that she was running her fingers up and down the desk as if she was playing the piano.

She nearly jumped out of her skin when she saw me because I was wearing a green garbage bag over my head with holes for the eyes and nose. It was too wet for her to come out, so I got the plant pot and climbed inside.

"Don't you have a raincoat?" she said as I struggled out of the garbage bag and got water all over her desk.

"My slicker was upstairs and I thought they might tell me not to go out," I said.

"Well, I'm glad you came over," she said. "I've been bored out of my mind."

"I came to invite you for Sunday dinner," I said. "We have our main meal at noon on Sunday. My brothers are less obnoxious than usual because Gran comes up from the city and Mum and Dad keep them under control."

"That sounds great," Dimsie said. "I'm sure my grandmother will let me. She'll be glad to get me out of the way."

"Your room is just as messy as mine," I said. There were dresses and shirts and pants in piles all over the floor and six pairs of different kinds of shoes lined up against the wall.

"I'm not usually this messy," she said, "but there's nowhere to hang anything up. I hate this room. It feels like a cage."

It really was a terrible room. The walls were bare but there were holes and marks all over them as if pictures had been taken down. There was a big square patch opposite the bed as if a big poster or a map had been taken down. I thought even Jenny wouldn't be able to fix up a room like that.

"Why is the closet all tied up?" I said.

There was a big closet with double doors along one side of the room, but someone had taken a bunch of thick string and wound it tightly around the door handles to tie them shut.

"I don't know," Dimsie said. "So many rooms and cupboards are locked up in this house. It's like Bluebeard's castle."

"Don't you wonder what's inside them?"

"Well, I've peeped through the keyholes in some of the rooms and all I can see is furniture covered up with white sheets. It's like a ghost house."

"I could cut the string off that door with my gardening clippers," I said. "We could see what's in there. That's if you aren't scared of what your grandmother would say."

"She wouldn't know," Dimsie said, "because she never comes down here. She can't manage the stairs because she has bad knees."

"Then I'll bring my clippers over tomorrow after supper," I said.

"I'll get some food," she said, "and we can have a picnic."

Then she asked me if I'd gone out to Peacehaven. She thought it was hilarious that I went out there and got insulted all the time.

"If you're so interested," I said, "why don't you come with me?"

"How would I get out there? I don't have a bike."

"You could borrow Jenny's," I said. "She wouldn't mind. I'll ask her mother tomorrow morning, then we can ride out together in the afternoon. You'll be able to see Miss Gwillam and the mouse house, and I'll introduce you to mean Mr. Martin."

"I'd love to," she said, "but I can't do it tomorrow because we're going down to the city."

"I thought you said your grandmother never leaves the house."

"She doesn't usually, but tomorrow we have to leave because some man's coming to work here."

"What kind of work?"

"Haven't a clue."

"Didn't you ask?"

"Yes, but she didn't answer. She doesn't answer a lot of my questions."

Then Dimsie asked me to tell her all the insulting things Mr. Martin had said.

"Well, I took him an old pair of Dad's slippers, and when I got them on his feet, he said he liked ones with holes in them so his feet could breathe. So I tried to take them off him but he wouldn't let me. He said he'd had enough aggravation without trying on shoes all afternoon."

"What a pain."

"He is, but I like reading his son's letters. If we have to do a report in social studies next year, I'm going to do one on Nunavut. They only have four hours of daylight up there now, and soon they won't have any. It'll be dark all the time."

"You've got it the wrong way round," Dimsie said. "It's in winter that it's dark for twenty-four hours. In summer it stays light all the time. I saw a show about it. It's too bad you don't watch TV more. You can learn a lot."

"Well, he lives up there," I said, "so he should know whether it's light or dark."

It really made me mad the way Dimsie thought she knew everything because she'd looked it up on the internet or seen a program on TV about it. I got up and started to pull the garbage bag over my head again.

"I have to get back," I said. "I have to write a letter."

"Don't eat any supper tomorrow so you'll have room for our picnic," she said."

I nodded. But I didn't tell her I planned to be back at The Meads long before supper time.

There was something funny going on in that house with its locked rooms and stuff covered up with sheets. I wondered why all the pictures had been taken down in Dimsie's room. Were they valuable paintings that her grandmother didn't want her to see? And I was really curious about what was going on in the house the next day while they were away in the city.

It was all very suspicious, and I planned to keep an eye on the house to see if I could find any clues about what was happening.

7
DETECTIVE WORK

I WENT BY The Meads on my way out to
Peacehaven the next morning. I rode all the way up
the driveway to the front door. The house was quiet
and dark and gloomy as usual. But there was no
man and nothing was going on that I could see, so
I turned around and left.

I'd picked a bouquet for Miss Gwillam and tied
it up with raffia the way they do at the flower shop.

"Why, Ellen, that's beautiful," she said when she
saw it. She went to the mouse house and took out
some tiny vases that were just big enough to hold a
small daisy and a sprig of the feverfew.

She was just taking the small flowers out of the
bouquet when she suddenly stopped.

"What's this I see?" she said, pointing at some blue flowers.

"It's catnip," I said.

"Oh, Ellen, how could you!" she said. "Don't you know better than to bring those flowers near Mousefield Park? Take the whole thing out of the room immediately." And she actually gave me a small push towards the door.

I took them into the staff kitchen where Kelly was having a coffee break. She looked up from her magazine.

"Oh, there you are," she said. "Mr. Martin was just asking for you. He's ornery as can be this morning. Wouldn't touch his breakfast, and I can't repeat what he called his tea."

"Kelly," I said, "why is everybody here so rude? I brought these flowers for Miss Gwillam and she practically threw me out of her room because of the catnip."

"You don't get any medals for helping out around here, that's for sure," Kelly said.

"Why do you work here, then?"

"Well, it's better than being stuck at a desk in an office. What I'd really like is real nursing, only you have to go to college for that, and I didn't finish high school. I'd meet plenty of young doctors in a hospital. And I like looking after people."

"Even when they're so mean?"

"Look, Ellen, you can't take it personally when they complain. It's not about you. A lot of them have serious illnesses. They don't feel good and all the aches and pains make them cranky. Plus they get frustrated because they can't do much for themselves. When they find fault with everything, it makes them feel a bit less helpless. You just have to let it go in one ear and out the other."

"That's what Dad says when Mum gets grumpy."

"Well, you know all about it then. Why don't you go and visit Mr. Martin? Maybe he'll drink some tea if you get it for him."

On the draining board there was a brown tea pot, the kind that Gran used, so I decided to make him a real pot of tea, the way Gran did.

I warmed the pot properly before I poured the boiling water over the tea bags. Then I got a cup and saucer and some milk, put them on a tray and carried them down the hall.

When I went into Mr. Martin's room, I noticed that he was wearing Dad's slippers.

"I made you a special pot of tea," I said. I put the tray down, poured out a cup and handed it to him.

"It's a bit early for tea," he said. I tried to let the remark go in one ear and out the other.

"At least it's hot," he said, as he took a sip.

"Mr. Martin," I said, "is Rupert married?"

"No. Maybe he never met the right gal up there."

"How old is he?"

"Next month's his forty-fifth birthday."

"That's pretty old," I said. "But if he came for a visit here and met the right girl…"

"Ellen, you're too young to be thinking like that. All you gals got only one thing on your minds. You watch too many soap operas."

"That's a stupid thing to say," I said. "I wasn't talking about myself. I was talking about a friend of mine."

I was so mad I was nearly shouting. I guess I forgot about letting things go in one ear and out the other.

"Yeah, right!" he said. "Got any more of that tea left?"

He seemed to think it was funny. The tea pot was cold and it needed a tea cozy, but he guzzled the tea down anyway.

As soon as he finished, I picked up the tray, took everything back to the kitchen, washed the cup and saucer and put them on the draining board. By the time I was through, I'd calmed down a bit.

Kelly came in just as I was leaving.

"Kelly," I said, "how would you feel about living in the Arctic?"

"Snow would be a change from all the rain we get around here, but I wouldn't like some of the stuff they eat. Caribou and seals."

"Rupert Martin isn't married," I said. "He never met the right girl."

"Probably inherited his dad's personality. How did the tea go over? Did he say thanks?"

"No," I said. "But he wanted a second cup."

"Wow, that's progress."

On the way home, I went by The Meads again. This time there was a big car outside the front door. I got off my bike and was just wondering what to do when the door opened and a man came out with two long black cases.

He was wearing a suit and a tie and he didn't look like a plumber or carpenter or someone who'd come to do work on the place. He put the cases down on the step, locked the door and put the key under a stone in the flower bed. Then he picked up the cases.

He was just walking back to his car when he saw me and he stopped. I knew he was thinking I'd seen him hide the key.

"It's all right," I said. "I just came to see Dimsie."

"Dimsie?"

"Mrs. Broster's granddaughter. She's my friend."

"There's nobody home. They've gone down to the city for the day."

"I know," I said. I could have bitten my tongue because I realized as soon as I said it that I'd contradicted myself. "I guess I'd better be going."

I'd reached the end of the driveway and gone up the road a little ways before I heard the car come down the driveway. It went off in the direction of the city.

I had a bad feeling the man would tell Mrs. Broster that I'd been snooping around the house.

Sure enough, when I went over to see Dimsie after supper, it was the first thing she asked me.

"Ellen, what were you doing at the house today when you knew we weren't here?" she said.

"I thought maybe you'd changed your mind about going down to the city," I said. It was a big fat lie and I felt bad saying it, but I couldn't very well admit that I was spying on them. "How did you know I was here?"

"My grandmother told me. The man who was here left her a note. He had to leave the key in a different place because you saw him hide it."

"What was he doing here?" I said.

"I don't know," Dimsie said. "My grandmother said to ask if you heard any noise."

As soon as she said that I remembered that when I was riding towards the house I'd heard a boing-boing, like the sound the bell on our deck makes when Dad's calling us up to the house. At the time I wondered if he was ringing for me to go home, but the sound wasn't coming from the right direction.

Then Dimsie started telling me what she'd done in the city, and how much smaller the museum and everything was than the one in Toronto. So I forgot about the man and the noise until later.

8
THE LOCKED CLOSET

I'D·TRIED NOT TO eat much at supper but it was hard because we were having pizza. It was still raining when I finished clearing up but I had my yellow slicker on this time when I crept out of the house. I also had a bag with a tea kettle and my garden clippers in it. I could hardly wait to start on the door handles and see what was in the closet, but as it turned out, I had to be patient because Dimsie had gone all out on the picnic.

She had candles so we could eat by candlelight, though when she lit them I thought it was more creepy than cozy because the candlelight threw these huge shadows on the walls. There was tons of food — a bag of Chinese chews, peanut butter cookies and some chocolate slices from a bakery, as well as sausage rolls and burritos and sushi. She must have spent her whole day in the city collecting food.

That was before she showed me the rest of the stuff she'd bought. She got a miniature silver piano for her charm bracelet, a beaded purse that she could hang around her neck, and another pair of sandals, even though she already had six pairs of shoes lined up by her bed. She also bought a dreamcatcher as a present for Uma.

"I got you a present, too," she said, and handed me a painted wooden doll. "It's a Russian doll. Go on, open it." It came apart and there was a smaller doll inside it. There were seven dolls in all, the last one really tiny.

"That's neat. Thanks," I said, though I'm not that keen on dolls.

"If you don't like it, you can give it away," she said. "That's okay with me."

"No, I really like it," I said quickly, "but wasn't it expensive?"

"Well, there aren't many shops out here," she said. "It's a real challenge to know what to spend your money on."

After I'd put the dolls back inside each other, we sat on the floor drinking hot chocolate and eating. We ate the cookies first, and then the sausage rolls and the burritos and the sushi last. After that we ate some more cookies. Then she asked me what I'd done at Peacehaven.

I told her about Miss Gwillam and the catnip, and about Mr. Martin and the slippers, and about my idea for Rupert Martin and Kelly. I'd also met a new couple called Mr. and Mrs. Renfrew. They were both in wheelchairs and always sat side by side doing a crossword puzzle or playing Scrabble. Their daughter was a teacher in Korea, and they showed me the presents she'd sent them — coasters and dolls and embroidered slippers, which they wouldn't even wear because they were too beautiful.

Finally we got around to the closet.

There were two doors, and the string that went round the handles holding them together was more like rope. At first I didn't think even the clippers would cut through it. But I managed to separate the different strands and chop through each one until I was finally able to throw open the door.

"Wow," we both said at the same time.

It was a walk-in closet, like a small room. There was a row of small filing cabinets, each with two drawers. On top of them were a lot of boxes and some books. At the sides of the closet there were rows of clothes on hangers.

The clothes were mostly long dresses in different kinds of beautiful material — silk and satin and lace — though there were long coats, too. Some of the dresses had beaded tops, and many of them were black but there were some green and blue ones, too. Underneath the dresses there were rows of shoes with high heels.

"They look like the pictures in Kelly's magazines," I said. "Was your grandmother a movie star or something?"

"Don't be ridiculous," Dimsie said. "She was a teacher."

"So these aren't her clothes."

Dimsie took down a dress and held it against her. It had a skirt with layer on layer of thin material like Gran's bathroom curtains, only green. The dress smelled like roses.

I opened the lid of one of the boxes on top of the filing cabinets. The inside of it was velvet, and on the velvet was a very sparkly necklace.

"Are those real diamonds?" Dimsie said. She dropped the dress and started taking the necklace out of the box. I opened another box and it had velvet inside, too, and a pearl necklace lying on the velvet.

"It's like Aladdin's cave," I said.

"More like pharoah's tomb," she said. "Help me

get this dress over my head, and then I'm going to put the necklace on. I wish there was a mirror in this room."

"Dimsie," I said, "let's find out what else is in the closet before we start trying stuff on."

It was getting late and I knew I'd have to leave soon, but I'd spotted a big picture leaning against the wall behind the dresses. It looked about as big as the bare patch on the wall opposite Dimsie's bed.

I managed to pull it out, and Dimsie helped me lean it up against the filing cabinets. Then we turned it around.

"Wow!" we both said together.

It was a painting of a woman. Her head filled almost the whole picture. She had long dark hair and half of her face was in shadow. She seemed to be looking right at us, and she had a kind of half smile on her face.

"Who is she?" I said.

"I don't know," Dimsie said.

For some reason we were both whispering.

"Is it your grandmother when she was younger?"

"She looks a bit like my grandmother, only I've seen photos of Granny Broster and her hair was fair before it turned gray. She doesn't look like anybody I know."

For a while neither of us said anything. It was very frustrating. I hated to leave just then but I knew I'd be in big trouble if I didn't get home soon. It was getting really dark.

"We can look at the rest of the stuff tomorrow," I said. "Should I tie the doors closed again?"

"No, leave them," she said. "I'll tie them up later."

I felt funny leaving the doors open and the string all cut up, because I wasn't at all convinced her grandmother wouldn't come downstairs. But there wasn't anything I could do, so we blew out the candles, and Dimsie helped me climb out of the window.

"See you tomorrow," I said.

"Hey, you forgot your present," she said, and she handed the Russian doll out of the window.

After I went to bed, I lay awake for hours thinking about the closet. I'd thought that we'd solve the mystery of Mrs. Broster's house when we opened the closet, but instead of solving anything we'd just stumbled on more mysteries.

When I'm trying to solve a problem, I usually make a list of the questions that need answering. I did this in my mind as I lay in bed.

Why did Dimsie's grandmother take that picture off the wall and lock it in a closet?

What was all that stuff in the closet? Did it belong to somebody or was it stolen?

If it did belong to somebody, was it to the woman in the picture?

Who was the woman in the picture?

What was the man doing at the house while Dimsie and her grandmother were in the city? Was he Mrs. Broster's partner in crime?

I must have fallen asleep while I was making my list, and I had one of the worst nightmares I ever had in my life. I was wandering through the long dark corridors of The Meads. As I went along, doors creaked open just a little, and I could see white forms moving in the rooms, holding lighted candles. I was searching for Dimsie, and I was very scared.

Suddenly a great bell like a church bell started to ring — ding dong, ding dong — and in the middle of the ringing I heard someone calling my name.

I sat up in a fright and threw off the blankets.

"Ellen," Dad was shouting. "Do you know what time it is?"

"I overslept," I said, as I staggered into the kitchen. "I had the worst nightmare."

It was after ten o'clock on Sunday morning and Gran had just arrived. She said bad dreams were usually caused by something you ate the night before. She said cheese always gave her a disturbed night. Tim said that was dyspepsia and there was a medicine you could get for it. Toby said it was acid reflux and you could get pills from the drugstore.

"We had pizza for supper," Mum said, "but Ellen didn't eat very much. I wondered at the time if your stomach was upset. Have you been eating between meals?"

"Not between meals," I said.

9
LUNCH AT THE FREMEDONS

"WE'RE HAVING A GUEST for lunch — a new friend of Ellen's," Mum told Gran.

Just then the doorbell rang and I went to let Dimsie in.

"Ellen, you'll never guess what I found — "

"Don't keep your friend standing on the door step," Mum called out, and then Tim and Toby came running to the door.

By the time Dimsie had been introduced to everyone, we had to go to the table. Mum sat at one end in her wheelchair and Dad sat at the other. Dimsie was between Gran and Tim, and Toby and I were on the other side of the table, so there was no way Dimsie and I could have a private conversation during lunch.

"Have you ever had scurvy?" Tim asked Dimsie, as Dad served a large salmon that was sitting on a bed of parsley and lemon slices. "Lemon slices are the best thing to cure it."

Dimsie said she hadn't had scurvy.

"Have you ever had worms?" Toby said.

"No," Dimsie said. "My friend's dog had worms, though. They had to take it to the vet to have it wormed."

"I ate an apple with a worm in it," Tim said, "but Dad won't take me to the doctor to get an x-ray."

"Maybe he should take you to the vet and get you wormed," I said.

"There are hookworms and ringworms and tapeworms," Toby said. "They cause weight loss, diarrhea and stomach cramps."

"Tapeworms can grow 25 feet long," Tim said. "You find the eggs on your stool."

"*In* your stool," I said.

"That's enough, Ellen," Dad said, picking on me as usual. "I think we've heard enough about worms."

"I don't want salmon if it's pink on the inside," Toby said. "I could get salmonella."

"You don't get salmonella from salmon," I said. "It's not like chicken, dummy. It's pink all the way through."

"I think we should explain the twins' preoccupation with disease to our guest," Dad said. "Toby and Tim are preparing for careers in medicine."

"That's because they've got a medical dictionary," I said. "I lent them a dollar for it, too, and I haven't got it back yet."

"Well, you get as much use from it as we do," Toby said. "More, in fact, because all the ice cream and candy you eat could cause a lot of illnesses. It was money well spent, Ellen."

"That's true," Gran said. "It was probably a wise investment. There should be a medical dictionary in every house. I always consult mine before I see my doctor, and I'm often able to come up with a correct diagnosis before she examines me."

"You often come up with a wrong one, too," Mum said. "Remember when you diagnosed yourself with a brain tumor?"

"According to my doctor, I was right to be alarmed," Gran said. "Vertigo can be a serious symptom."

"And what about the time you told her you needed a pacemaker because your heart was pounding? It turned out you were drinking enough coffee to make an elephant keel over."

"We have a very unhealthy lifestyle in this family," Tim said. "It's a miracle I'm still alive."

"It's our bedtime," Toby said. "We go to bed too

early. If you spend too much time in bed you get bedsores. There are four stages of bedsores and we're at the third stage already. Our skin's already red and blistered and peeling. Soon deep craters will appear, and then — "

"If your skin's red and peeling, it's because you don't wear sunscreen when you go out in the sun," Mum said. "That *is* serious, and you have only yourself to blame."

"Then we're at risk for Weaver's Bottom," Tim said.

"Goodness, what's that?" Gran said.

"People get it if they sit for a long time in one position like we do in school," Tim said. "It's a swelling and pain in the hips. I found out about it when I was looking up Mr. Banks' bursitis. I realized I've had it for a long time and it's getting worse all the time."

"I hope all this talk isn't putting Dimsie off her lunch," Gran said, turning to Dimsie. "How is your grandmother? I remember how hard she used to work raising money for the symphony."

"I didn't know you knew Mrs. Broster," I said.

"I didn't know her personally," Gran said. "Everyone knew *of* her, and looked up to her, because she was so…"

We all waited for Gran to finish her sentence.

Instead she made the clucking noise she makes when she's knitting and she's dropped a stitch. She smiled at Dimsie and didn't say any more.

After a while, I brought out the dessert plates and set a large Black Forest cake in the middle of the table. It was decorated with whipped cream and cherries.

"As usual Gran's brought a wonderful cake," Dad said. "What a pity that those who suffer from high cholesterol or Weaver's Bottom won't be able to enjoy it."

"Ellen better not have any," Toby said, "because of her acid reflux. That's what's been giving her nightmares and making her crabby lately. It disrupts your sleep because when you lie down the acid in your stomach starts to come right back up — "

"A little of what you fancy does you good," Gran said quickly.

"And what medical book is the source of that wonderful advice?" Mum said.

It seemed like hours before lunch was finished, but finally Dimsie and I were able to get our bikes and set out for Peacehaven. The rain had stopped and the sun had come out by the time we left the house.

"So what did you find out?" I said at last.

"There was this book lying on top of the filing cabinets, and it had a bookplate in it…"

"A bookplate?"

"You know, like people paste in the front of books to say it's theirs. Well, there was this book-plate inside and it said 'EX LIBRIS Catriona Broster.'"

"Ex libris?"

"That means 'from the library of,' and Catriona Broster was my mother's name. There was tons of piano music, too, and it had her name written on it. The woman in the painting — I'm sure that was my mother, and I think all the clothes and stuff belonged to her…"

"Wow!" I said, trying to sound amazed. Actually I wasn't all that surprised. It was one of the things that had gone through my mind while I was having a sleepless night.

"And those filing cabinets are full of letters."

"Did you read them?" Now I was getting excited.

"Well, there were so many and it was getting really late so I tied the closet back up like you showed me. But when you come over tonight we can open the closet and read the stuff in the files."

We were almost at Peacehaven just then. I looked up the road and I knew immediately that something unusual was going on, because there were so many cars in the parking lot.

10
A HUNDRED YEARS OLD

WHEN WE WENT IN, there was a crowd of people in the lobby and TV room. They were all really dressed up, and some of the women were even wearing big hats with wide brims. Mrs. Fisher, the superintendent, was going around shaking hands with everybody.

"It's Mrs. McCrorie's hundredth birthday," Kelly told us. "They're going to read out a message from the Governor General."

Mrs. McCrorie was in the middle of a crowd, sitting in a wheelchair with a shawl draped around it so that it looked like an armchair. She either had a new hairdo or she was wearing a wig, and someone had put blush on her cheeks. Beside her on the table was an oblong birthday cake with about a million candles on it, a bowl of pink punch, a pile of presents and some flower arrangements — the real kind that you get at the florist.

A man with a camera on his shoulder was standing nearby, and a young woman reporter with a notebook was trying to interview her.

"Can you tell us the secret of your longevity?" the journalist asked.

"No, I don't need to go to the lavatory," Mrs. McCrorie said. "I just went."

"She wants to know how come you've lived so long, Gertie?" Mrs. Fisher shouted in her ear. There was a sudden hush while everyone waited for the answer.

"Bananas," she said.

"She's gone bananas," a little boy said, and his father slapped him on the ear.

"It's true," Kelly said. "She goes berserk if we forget to give her a banana every day for her breakfast. It has to be overripe, too."

"A banana a day keeps the undertaker away," a man with a bow tie said, and some people glared at him.

"Time for the cake!" Mrs. Fisher said.

They wheeled Mrs. McCrorie around to the table, where three people were lighting all the candles. A photographer got ready to take a picture.

"Get one of those girls to stand beside her," he said, pointing to where Dimsie and I were standing. "The pretty one."

"Come and help your grandmother blow out her candles," a woman in a hat with a lot of flowers on it said to Dimsie.

Dimsie looked a bit startled but she went up and blew out some of the candles while the man took a lot of pictures. Everyone sang "Happy Birthday," but Mrs. McCrorie just sat there stroking Dimsie's hair like she really was her granddaughter.

"Bagpipes," she said. "Give us a tune on the bagpipes, Bonnie."

"My name's Dimsie, and I play the piano," Dimsie said.

"Well, play her a tune on the piano," Mrs. Fisher said. So Dimsie went over to the piano and played some Scottish song. Then she went on playing other pieces while Kelly and Mrs. Fisher and another helper passed out pieces of cake and glasses of punch. The birthday girl fell fast asleep.

When I'd eaten my cake, I decided to go and visit Mr. Martin. I knew he wasn't supposed to have cake so I grabbed one of the flower arrangements from the table.

"There's a lot of racket for a Sunday afternoon," he said. "Who's that thumping on the piano?"

"A friend of mine. They're celebrating Mrs. McCrorie's hundredth birthday."

"What's to celebrate just because you hang around for a hundred years? Besides, it's not a party they're having. It's a publicity stunt." He seemed more crabby than usual.

"I brought you some flowers," I said. He took the flower arrangement and sniffed it.

"What are they up to now?"

"They're eating birthday cake, and there's a photographer taking pictures."

"Of course there is. Old Fish Face never misses a chance for a photo op. They put pictures in the paper so everyone thinks we're having a ball out here in this dump. Well, I don't want any part of it."

"I don't either."

"That so?" he said. "What got your goat?"

"They said I'm not pretty."

"Are you?"

"No. But they don't have to rub it in."

"You don't need a pretty face. You got brains."

"I thought you said I was ignorant and didn't know anything."

"Anybody that asks as many questions as you do isn't going to stay ignorant for long."

"But suppose nobody gives me the right answers?" I said.

"You don't need anybody to give you the answers. You're smart enough to figure them out for yourself. Just keep your mouth shut and your ears open."

Before I could say anything, he handed me back the flowers.

"Don't think much of these. They don't have any smell to them."

"Hot house flowers never do. I'll bring you more from our garden."

"Think you could get me a wad of cotton or some earplugs to shut out that din on the piano before I burst an eardrum?"

"We have some earmuffs that Mum wore in the garden when our neighbors were using a weed-eater," I said. "They work really well."

"See if you can bring them before the warbling starts on Wednesday."

The music had stopped, so I went out to find Dimsie.

"Where did you disappear to?" she said, as we went out to get our bikes. "Were you visiting that rude old man?"

"He's not all that rude."

"I really like the people here," she said. "They clapped their hands off when I'd finished playing. And the photographer took more pictures. They're

going to be in next Sunday's paper. I'm really looking forward to seeing them because I'm very photogenic. I'll send copies to Uma and my dad. And
Mrs. Fisher invited me to go back and play the
piano. She said I'm very talented."

I felt like telling her one person wanted earplugs
to shut out her playing.

All the way home, she went on and on about the
compliments she'd got on her playing and her hair
and her clothes. She'd got all dressed up for lunch,
even though I told her a T-shirt and jeans would be
okay, and she was wearing the sandals she'd
bought in the city, even though she knew we'd be
riding our bikes.

She seemed to have forgotten all about the closet, though she did tell me to come over as I soon as
I could after supper.

I wasn't even sure I wanted to go.

When I got home, Gran was in the kitchen,
opening and shutting drawers.

"Have you seen the tea cozy, Elinor?" she asked
Mum.

"Ellen was looking for it the other day," Mum
said, then they both looked at me.

"There's been a general migration of items from
our kitchen to Peacehaven," Dad said. "We've lost
to date — two flower vases, an inflatable cushion, a

tea strainer, and now the tea cozy. It's a good thing the furniture's too big to carry over there."

"Why did you stop what you were saying about Mrs. Broster when we were having lunch?" I asked Gran.

"Oh, I didn't want to embarrass your friend by mentioning a painful subject," she said.

"What painful subject?"

"Well, there was some kind of accident involving Mrs. Broster's daughter, and people said she was never the same after that."

"What happened?"

"I'm not entirely sure," Gran said. "It was several years ago, and it happened somewhere down east. I seem to recall it involved a traffic accident."

"Can you phone me, if it comes back to you?" I said.

"Oh, Ellen, it's water under the bridge," Gran said. "Mrs. Broster has obviously gone on with her life. And having her pretty granddaughter with her for the summer must be cheering her up. She has such nice manners."

Jenny was pretty and talented and had nice manners, but she didn't go around bragging about how photogenic and talented she was. I was pretty fed up with Dimsie Fairchild. I felt like writing to Jenny instead of going over to The Meads. I wanted to tell her what had happened at Peacehaven and how snobby and spoiled and rich Dimsie was.

Then I thought if I got started on Dimsie, I'd be writing for hours. And thinking about Dimsie made me think about the closet again, and the book she'd found and the letters in the filing cabinets. I wondered if she was sitting at her desk reading the letters.

Finally, my curiosity got the better of me, and I thought I might as well go over and see what she was doing.

11
CLIPPINGS

THERE WAS A LIGHT on in her room, but Dimsie wasn't sitting at her desk. When I peered in the window I saw her sitting on the floor. There were papers scattered all around her and she was reading.

I tapped on the window softly at first because I didn't want to wake Mrs. Broster, and then louder.

Finally, Dimsie looked up.

"What took you so long?" she said as she helped me climb over the window sill. "I thought you were never coming. You won't believe the interesting stuff I've found about my mother."

I sat down on the floor and she started showing me bits from the letters she was reading.

"These are letters my mother wrote to my grandmother when she was away at school," Dimsie said. "Listen to this."

Dear Mumbo,

I went to my audition last night. What an experience! I had to take a cab to the conservatory. When I got there I found the auditions were being held in another building several blocks away so I arrived with cold stiff hands. I just had time to take off my coat before I was sent into the judging room. There was a condescending young man draped over a piano bench, a fat pasty-faced man, and another man about thirty-five. I remembered Caroline C. saying, 'imagine them in their underwear,' and that helped...

"Isn't that amazing, Ellen? My mother was a pianist. And isn't that a coincidence, finding a letter about an audition she had when she in high school just when I'm worrying about my audition? I feel as if she wrote this letter specially to me."

"Did she pass the audition?" I said.

"She doesn't say. She just says that she went

back to school and all her friends tried to cheer her up. She says, 'Anyway I tried, I cried, it was an experience. I'll keep trying, and I'll go for it next year.'"

She was all lit up about her mother's letters.

"What's that?" I said, pointing to a big album on the floor next to the files.

"It's a scrapbook full of articles about my mother. She was really good. She performed in public."

"That explains why she had all those long dresses," I said, thinking that at least one of the mysteries was cleared up. But Dimsie didn't seem to be thinking about any of that. She was so excited about her mother being a pianist.

"She won a scholarship to the Julliard in New York. It's one of the best music schools in the world. And then she went to the Chopin Academy in Poland. Can you believe it? She played Chopin! Oh, I wish I'd known her."

"I guess she did pass the audition, then."

"Maybe she didn't. Maybe she tried again the next year and passed then," Dimsie said. "Oh, I wish I could talk to her."

For a while we sat side by side, leaning against Dimsie's bed with the scrapbook on our knees, turning the pages together, reading the articles from the paper and looking at the pictures. The photos weren't very clear, and most of them were taken from the side when she was playing the piano, so you couldn't see exactly what she looked like, except that she had long dark hair.

When we got to the end of the pages with clippings, there were a lot of empty pages. There was also an envelope at the back of the book with some more clippings stuffed in. We pulled them out and spread them on the floor.

We looked at them for a while without saying anything. Dimsie had gone very quiet.

"These are about the accident," she said at last.

"Well, go on," I said. "Let's read them."

She looked as if she couldn't make up her mind whether to read them or not. Finally she read the first one, passed it to me and looked at me while I read it.

PIANIST IN MINOR ACCIDENT
Local pianist Catriona Broster was involved in a minor collision on Thursday night at the intersection of Avenue Road and Woodside. The car she was driving ran a red light and hit a vehicle in the oncoming traffic. Both vehicles were damaged but none of the passengers sustained injuries. Broster suffered slight shock and was taken to the hospital overnight for observation. Alcohol was not

involved. Broster is expected to be released from hospital in the next day or two.

"But you told me she was killed in the accident," I said.

"Well, that's what my dad and my grandmother told me," Dimsie said. "Read this one."

LOCAL PIANIST DISAPPEARS
Catriona Broster, the local musician who was hospitalized with minor injuries after a car accident, disappeared from her hospital room late Thursday evening. It was first thought that she had felt well enough to return home and had unadvisedly left the hospital. But her family reports they have received no word from her. Authorities fear that she may have been suffering from amnesia and wandered out into the streets. Police have issued descriptions of her. Broster, well known in local musical circles, left wearing only sandals and a borrowed raincoat over her hospital gown. Anyone with information about Broster or about anyone resembling her is asked to contact the police.

Dimsie watched me again while I read the article, and then she read the next ones and passed them over.

STILL NO SIGN OF MISSING WOMAN
There is still no sign of Catriona Broster, the pianist who disappeared from her hospital bed over a week ago. Several reports of a disoriented woman wandering near the beach have led police to think that she might have wandered into the water and drowned. No body has been recovered. Police are continuing their investigation.

POLICE DISCONTINUE SEARCH FOR MISSING PIANIST
Police have finally given up their search for Catriona Broster.

MEMORIAL CONCERT FOR MISSING MUSICIAN CANCELLED
The memorial concert that was planned for Catriona Broster, the pianist who disappeared from her hospital bed where she was undergoing treatment for shock after a traffic accident, has been cancelled. Organizers

announced today that family members felt that any kind of memorial was highly inappropriate. Certain family members still hold out hope that Broster might be alive. The pianist's mother has offered a reward of $50,000 for anyone coming forward with information about her daughter. It is understood that she is spearheading an extensive search.

"It's terrible to think she drowned," Dimsie said.

"But they don't know what happened," I said. "Nobody knows. They're just guessing."

"Do you know exactly what amnesia is?" she said.

"It's something to do with not remembering things, like Alzheimer's. The twins say Gran has it. They got a test out of a book that tells whether you're likely to come down with it. They want to give it to Gran, but Mum won't let them. Gran's very touchy about her memory."

"Well, I want to find out more about amnesia. I have to find out how my mother died. I'll go down to the library tomorrow and look it up on one of their computers."

I felt bad leaving Dimsie after she'd gone quiet

and sad, and I knew she was thinking about her mother who might have drowned.

After I climbed back out of the window, I saw her go back to sit on the floor. I left her reading her mother's letters.

12
AMNESIA

WE SPENT MOST OF the next morning trying to find a computer so that we could look up amnesia on the internet. Dad won't let us kids anywhere near his computer, Anne and Cathy weren't home, and both the computers in the library were down.

"You'd think they'd be able to get computers that work," I said, "with all the money they rake in on fines."

"I can't believe the way people live in this dump," Dimsie said. "There isn't even an internet café."

Finally I decided I would try to borrow the twins' medical dictionary.

"We need it all the time," Tim said. "What you don't realize is that a lot of people around here ask us for help when they get sick. We're busy all day long."

"Mrs. Banks says she'll give us a hundred dollars if we can cure her migraines," Toby said. "We've got a lot of money riding on this, Ellen."

"I'll give you fifty cents if you let me borrow it for half an hour," I said. They were saving up to buy a blood-pressure machine and a stethoscope.

"Fifty cents isn't much," Tim said. "The equipment we need is really expensive. A blood-pressure kit costs thirty dollars."

"Anyway, we can't do it just now. We have a patient waiting to see us."

When I caught up with them later, they were in the drugstore arguing with the pharmacist. Toby was carrying the dictionary.

"How many times have I told you two to stop playing with the blood-pressure machine," Rob was saying. "It's not a toy."

"I know it's not a toy," Tim said, "I was testing my blood pressure. High blood pressure's very serious in kids our age."

"You've tested it at least once a day this week. And this is the second time you've tested it today. And yesterday you were eating a muffin at the same time. People have been complaining about the crumbs all over the place."

"What you don't understand, Rob, is that blood pressure changes with the time of day and whether a meal was just eaten. That's why you have to test it more than once."

"Well, I don't want you testing it for the rest of the week. Is that clear?"

"If I have a stroke, you'll be sorry," Tim said.

"Don't count on it."

"Tim," I said, "if you let me have the dictionary for ten minutes, I'll give you a dollar for your blood-pressure kit."

"You probably won't understand the words when you look something up," Toby said.

"If you need any explaining, it'll cost you another dollar," Tim said.

I ended up paying a dollar to borrow the book for ten minutes and a dime to photocopy one page, but I got the entry I wanted.

AMNESIA, a loss of memory caused by brain damage or by severe emotional stress. ANTEROGRADE AMNESIA is the loss of memory of the events that occur after an injury. RETROGRADE AMNESIA is the loss of memory for events occurring before a set time in a patient's life, often before the event that caused the amnesia. The condition may result from disease, brain injury, or an emotional injury.

I gave the book back to the twins and left them still arguing with Rob.

"High blood pressure runs in our family," Toby said. "Our dad takes pills for it every morning."

"If I were your dad, I'd be taking pills for high blood pressure, too," Rob said. "Now, buzz off."

When I walked by the Creamery, Cathy Banks was sitting outside reading the paper at a table. She waved me over.

"Hey, Ellen," she said, "I was hoping to run into you. Jenny called her mom last night and asked about you. She said she hasn't heard a word from you. What've you been up to?"

"Mostly going out to Peacehaven," I said. "I've started a long letter but I haven't finished it. I'll finish it tonight and send it off tomorrow. Cathy, do you know anything about amnesia?"

"Sure," Cathy said. "People turn up on the streets and don't know who they are or how they got there, or where they came from in the first place."

"What happens to them?"

"Our investigative unit usually tries to locate their families."

"What if the police don't find them?"

"They can end up sleeping on the streets where they get robbed. They can get pneumonia, too, if it's really cold. But you don't have to worry if they're in Peacehaven. They look after them pretty well there, I've heard."

"I know."

"Anne's sending a package off to Jenny tomorrow," Cathy said, "so if you have anything you want to send along just bring it over. Or you could give it to the twins to bring over. They're giving Anne and me a test tonight to see if we're likely to come down with Alzheimer's."

"They gave that test to Dad," I said. "He flunked it, and now they think they'll have to quit school and look after him."

"Is that what's bothering you, Ellen? Worrying about your dad?"

"Oh, no, I'm not worried about Dad."

"I expect you're missing Jenny. We are, too. But cheer up. It won't be too long before she's home."

"I know," I said. "I'll finish that letter."

I felt a bit guilty because I wasn't actually missing Jenny. I was too busy thinking about Dimsie and her mother. But talking about Peacehaven reminded me that I had to get out there after lunch to take Mr. Martin the earmuffs.

Dimsie came with me, and we talked about amnesia as we rode along.

"People forget everything that happened to them before the thing that caused the amnesia," I said.

"Maybe my mother forgot she had a baby," Dimsie said.

"Maybe she didn't even know where she lived or what her own name was," I said. I remembered what Cathy had told me about people with amnesia living on the street, but I didn't say anything about that.

"I wonder why they never told me about her," Dimsie said.

I wondered about that, too, and it raised a lot of questions in my mind, but Dimsie didn't seem to be as suspicious and nosy as me.

After a while, she got onto what she'd found out from the letters, and how happy she was that her mother was so talented. I was glad she'd cheered up, though when we came back from Peacehaven, she was disappointed by the afternoon.

"I played them my recital pieces, but all they wanted to hear were the same old Scottish songs over and over again. It got pretty boring."

"Well, I love hearing you play the Chopin," I

said. "You could play it over and over and I'd never get tired of it."

"Why don't we have another picnic tonight?" she said. "Bring the hot chocolate and I'll get the food, and we can look at the stuff in the closet."

"Okay," I said.

13
ALARMING NEWS

I WAS STILL THINKING about Dimsie's mum when something else happened. Something very bad.

I heard the news when I ran into Higg at the supermarket. I'd picked out shortbread cookies for Mr. Martin from the various kinds of diabetic cookies available, six bran muffins and a packet of prunes for the Renfrews, and a box of Lemon Zinger tea for Miss Gwillam and the mice.

"Good grief, Ellen," Higg said, looking at the cart. "How many people are you shopping for at Peacehaven?"

"Just three here," I said. "Then I have to go over to the post office to buy some stamps for the Renfrews."

"That can't leave you much time for gardening."

It was true. Between going back and forth to Peacehaven and seeing Dimsie in the evenings, I hardly had time for anything else. I hadn't even cashed in my book certificate yet, and I still hadn't finished my letter to Jenny.

"It's okay," I said. "But I don't know who will do all these errands once school starts."

"Well, you don't have to worry about that," Higg said. "Didn't you hear the news on the radio this morning? The government is planning to shut down Peacehaven."

"It can't do that," I said. "Where will everybody go?"

"There are more modern facilities in the city. Some will find places there, I expect, and some will just have to make other arrangements. Or their families will."

"But a lot of them don't have families. Or if they do they're far away in other countries. Peacehaven's their home. They can't just throw them out."

"It's an old building, Ellen, and apparently it's not efficient to run. It needs a new roof, and the cost of that is huge."

"Can't they have bake sales and raise money for

a new roof the way the churches and the Boy Scouts do?"

"It would take more than a few bake sales to raise enough money to renovate that place," he said. "And I certainly don't have the time with Thumper to look after, and a new book coming out."

"Do the people at Peacehaven know about it?" I asked.

"If they haven't heard already, they soon will," Higg said.

I went straight out to Peacehaven, and when I walked in with my groceries, everyone had heard.

"This isn't just a seniors' home," Kelly said. "It's like a second home to me. I've never worked anywhere else since I quit high school. I've never done anything but look after old people. I don't know what else I would do."

Mr. Martin was sitting alone as usual. His window was slightly open, and a breeze was blowing in off the lake.

"Good thing you got me those earmuff things, Ellen," he said. "I'll sure need them in the city with traffic honking and sirens going all hours of the day and night. Maybe you could get me a face mask next so I won't have to breathe all the pollution."

"The mice are very upset, Ellen," Miss Gwillam said. "I don't think they can adjust to living in a big city. They're country mice. You can tell by looking at their beautiful long tails. And there are so many dangers in the city. Mousetraps. Cats…"

"There are cats in the country," I said. "Didn't their parents —?"

"Please, Ellen," Miss Gwillam said, putting her finger to her lips. "I told you never to refer to that unfortunate event in their hearing."

"Oh, Ellen," Mrs. Renfrew said. "It's a good thing you got stamps. I need to write to our daughter about this."

"Yoicks!" I said. "I forgot the stamps. I was so shocked when I heard the news that I came straight here. But I'll bring the stamps out this afternoon, and then I'll take the letter and mail it."

Back home I leaped off my bicycle and stomped straight to Dad's study and banged on the door.

"What is it, Ellen?" Dad said, looking up from his computer. "Can it wait? I'm just in the middle of something."

"It's Peacehaven," I said. "The government's going to close it down…"

"Ah, yes, I did hear something about that on the radio this morning."

"Well, it's not fair. All the old people will get

thrown out and have to pack up their stuff and have nowhere to go…"

"Your Peacehaven friends are not going to end up on the street. There are other retirement homes…"

"That's not the point. It's their *home*. And besides, the nurses and the cooks and all the others will lose their jobs. How would you like it if the government came and said they were shutting down our house and kicking us out and we had to find somewhere else to live? We have to do something."

"Calm down, Ellen," Dad said. "It is regrettable, but there's very little you or I can do about it. We weren't very successful, you remember, the last time we tried to stop something disgraceful from happening. After all our hard work a subdivision is still going up on top of our aquifer. Our water supply is being jeopardized, the inlet is being polluted, and all the developers, real estate agents and contractors are merrily making a fortune. "

"But you said we didn't waste our time. You said it was important to try to stop people from doing bad things."

"Well, yes, I did. But you have to keep in mind the old lifeboat example."

"What's that?"

"When you're on a lifeboat and many people are drowning, you can't rescue them all. You have to decide which ones to save. In other words, you can't take up every deserving cause. You only have the energy for one or two."

"That's not logical, Dad. It's a false analogy."

"You may be right there, Ellen. Well, I'll give this situation some thought. And now, let me get back to work. We'll discuss it later."

When Dad says he'll think about something, it usually means he'll forget about it. I was just heading to the door when he called out after me.

"Ellen, have you seen those old slippers of mine? I've been looking for them everywhere."

I just kept on going.

"Do you think your daughter will do something?" I asked the Renfrews when I took them the stamps. I thought that if the government got letters with foreign stamps on them, they might open them right away and change their minds about closing Peacehaven.

"Oh, no, Ellen," Mrs. Renfrew said. "She's teaching in Korea. She has her own problems, I'm sure, and I don't want her to worry about us. She did make me promise to write and tell her everything, but I always make my letters sound cheerful."

"Don't you think we should write and tell your

son? Maybe he can do something. After all, he's a policeman," I said to Mr. Martin.

"He's got his hands full in the Arctic," Mr. Martin said. "There's plenty of crime to fight up there." He seemed too grumpy to write a letter, so I wrote it myself.

Dear Mr. Rupert Martin,

My name is Ellen Fremedon and I am the girl who has been helping your father write his letters. We got some very bad news today. The government is going to shut down Peace-haven. All the seniors will get moved down to the city. This is their home and they like it here and they don't want to go somewhere else. If you know someone in the government, please write a letter telling them not to shut this place down.

Yours truly,
Ellen

I always give Mr. Martin's letters to Kelly to mail, so I told her I'd written this one myself, and asked her to send it Express.

"Express is too expensive," she said, "and it probably won't get there any quicker. I'll do it like I do all the others."

It was all so annoying. Everybody thought the government was doing something wrong, but they were all too selfish to do anything about it. Dad was always lecturing us about concern for other people, and good deeds being their own reward, but when it came right down to it, when somebody needed help, all he could think about was an old pair of slippers he hadn't worn for months. And Higg never had time for anything except Thumper and writing poetry. He wasn't even singing at Peacehaven anymore. Dimsie didn't care. She was all wrapped up in her mother's letters and thinking about her music.

"Oh, that's too bad," she said when I told her. "I'll play them something extra special next time I go over. What about 'Auld Lang Syne'?"

I thought it would take more than a few soppy old songs to save Peacehaven.

14
HUNGER STRIKE

"GRAN," I SAID AT lunch the next Sunday, "how long did it take the suffragettes to get the government to let women vote in elections?"

"Over sixty years, my dear," Gran said. "Isn't it incredible that it should have taken so long for them to get something that was so reasonable?"

"Tell about the ones that got trampled to death by the king's horse," Tim said.

"That was only one person," Gran said. "Emily Wilding Davison. She died tragically after throwing herself in front of the king's horse at a famous race."

"Fortunately, the horse and the jockey were unhurt," Mum said.

"Why this sudden interest in the suffrage movement?" Gran said.

"Ellen's upset because the provincial government intends to close down Peacehaven and demolish the building," Dad said. "But I very much doubt that the methods of the suffragettes can be used in this case."

"Well, something should be done," Gran said. "It's outrageous to shut down Peacehaven. What will happen to the people who live there?"

"They'll be moved to the city," Dad said. "It's more cost effective to have them in central locations rather than in small facilities dotted throughout the province."

"But many of them have lived in the Cowichan Valley for years. And what about the staff?"

"They'll have to find other jobs," Dad said. "That won't be easy, of course. I hope there'll be public outcry, but I'm far too busy myself at the moment to get involved. And, frankly, after our attempt to protect our water supply, I have little confidence in bringing about change."

"But you have to try to stop things that are wrong, even if you don't succeed. That's what you said before. What else did the suffragettes do, Gran?" I said.

"First they marched and made peaceful protests. And eventually they came up with one very effective weapon — the hunger strike. They were the first to use it as a — ”

“Mother, please. The children are at an impressionable age. This is not an appropriate subject,” Dad said.

“You said we should ask about anything we didn’t understand,” Tim said.

“I very much doubt that these three would have the willpower to stop eating,” Mum said.

“I could stop eating certain things,” Tim said. “Like Brussels sprouts, and Ellen’s gravy, and turnips.”

“You can’t just stop eating things you don’t like,” I said. “Nobody’s going to care if they see a headline in the paper that says, ‘Tim Fremedon Refuses to Eat Brussels Sprouts.’”

“What if we stop eating all our vegetables except peas?” Toby said.

“You have to stop eating *everything*.”

“Mrs. Pankhurst wouldn’t even take a drop of water,” Gran said. “She nearly died on one occasion.”

“Mother, please,” Dad said. “Let’s not pursue this subject.”

“It’s not pleasant, but it’s history, and the children should know about it,” Gran said.

"Cutting certain things out of your diet can cause serious problems," Tim said. "If you don't drink milk you get cavities, and if you don't have enough salt, you get goiter."

"Nobody gets goiter these days," I said. "And that includes Mrs. Fenwick. She's freaking out because you told her she's got it."

"Well, she looks like she's got it, and she doesn't eat salt because of her blood pressure," Tim said.

"I warned you not to try to diagnose the neighbors' ailments, especially when it involves their physical appearance," Dad said.

"Mrs. Fenwick has quite a prominent double chin," Mum explained to Gran.

"She has three chins," Tim said, "and that's sure a sign of goiter."

"It's a common problem with elderly ladies," Gran said, pulling her scarf up underneath her chin. "But how rude of Tim to mention it."

"Mr. Banks didn't mind when I said he's probably got gout because he has a red nose," Tim said. "He said I just saved him a trip to the doctor's office, and Mrs. Banks said I hit the nail on the head."

"Somebody's going to hit you on the head one of these days," I said. "And you'll need a trip to the doctor's office."

"Watch your tongue, Ellen," Dad said.

"If hunger strikes helped the suffragettes get votes for women, maybe they can stop the government from closing down Peacehaven," I said.

"Sometimes the prison authorities had to force-feed the suffragettes," Gran said. "It was a very ugly business involving tubes — "

"Please, Mother," Dad said.

"Do you have to be in prison to start a hunger strike?" Tim said. "Or can you just do it in your own home?"

"Perhaps we can think of a better way to protest the closing down of Peacehaven," Dad said. He put down his knife and fork, as if he'd lost his appetite.

"Dimsie Fairchild says that if this happened in Toronto, people would take to the streets in protest."

"We could take to the streets in protest."

"There aren't any streets in this dump," I said. "Basically there's only one main street."

"Well, we could take to it," Tim said. "We could get Sean Floyd to bring his drum. It makes a lot of noise."

"There's a meeting of the community council this week," Mum said. "It's to discuss the feasibility of a new swimming pool, but perhaps you could interest them in defending Peacehaven."

"You could try," Dad said, "but if you make a presentation to the community council you'd better be well prepared. It's a very acrimonious group."

"What's acrimonious?" Tim said.

"Look it up," Mum said, sounding as crabby as Dad.

"You should start by listing as many reasons as possible for keeping Peacehaven open," Dad said.

"It's not in the dictionary," Tim said, flipping through his medical dictionary.

"It's not a disease, dummy," I said. "You have to look it up in the regular dictionary."

"It shouldn't be hard to come up with some very strong arguments," Dad said. "I can think of several already. If Peacehaven closes, jobs will be lost. Many seniors are close to their families here. Those seniors from elsewhere have visitors and that brings business to Partridge Cove. They eat at the restaurant and they buy things in the stores. The seniors have served their communities during their lifetime and now it's the community's turn to care for them. And there must be a great many other reasons that escape my mind just now."

"You might ask the seniors and staff for their input," Gran said.

"And don't forget to make a list of reasons

against keeping the place open. That will help you to anticipate hostile questions," Dad said.

"I believe you'll need more than facts and figures and logic when you make your presentation," Mum said. "You'll have to capture the imagination of the group by describing the actual people who will be affected. People are often moved more by touching stories than by arguments."

"I think Ellen's going to have her work cut out," Gran said.

They all looked at me and I realized they were all great at giving advice but they weren't going to do a darn thing. I was on my own and I wouldn't be getting any help from anyone.

"I'll start this afternoon," I said. "I'll go out there and interview all the seniors."

15
COMMUNITY COUNCIL

IT WAS A LOT HARDER preparing the presentation for the community council than I thought it would be, and I wasted a lot of time interviewing people. Mum had said that the residents themselves would probably give me really moving arguments for staying in Partridge Cove.

It's true they talked my ears off when I asked why they wanted to stay at Peacehaven, but their arguments were not exactly useful.

"Why, Ellen, the reasons are obvious," Miss Gwillam said. "Jessie, Jemima, Japonica, Josephine and Jasmine are field mice. They don't mind visiting the city on occasion, but they certainly don't want to live there. People talk about the advantages of city life — the fine houses, all the different kinds of cheese available and so on. But they enjoy country life — walking, gardening and getting plenty of fresh air. Mousefield Park has been in their family for generations. Their parents and grandparents are buried in the garden. Living in a high-rise apartment would be horrible. Besides, think of the dangers — gangs of rats, traffic…"

"If I lived in the city," Mr. Martin said, "a lot of boring people would be dropping in. My nephew would come with his kids, and they get on my nerves."

"I thought you were all alone in the world," I said.

"I should be so lucky."

Only the Renfrews gave me something useful. They said that the newer facilities separate the men from the women, and they were afraid they would be put in separate rooms on different floors. They had been together for over fifty years, and it would break their hearts if they couldn't go on living together.

I figured the crowd at the council meeting would be shocked to think of people being treated like that.

I was so nervous on the night of the meeting

that I couldn't eat. Mum and Dad had given me lots of ideas and read my presentation, and they kept telling me I was well prepared and had nothing to worry about. Dimsie hadn't given me any ideas but she wanted to come to the meeting to see what happened. Everyone except Mum was going along to support me.

I decided to run through my speech one more time before we left.

"The only thing you have to worry about is your audience," Dad said. "There are sometimes hecklers, though I trust they'll show some restraint when a young person is speaking."

"What's hecklers?" Tim said.

"People who shout out questions and make rude remarks," Dad said.

"Ellen should read her speech again and let us heckle her for practice," Tim said.

"I get enough practice with hecklers from you two every day," I said.

When we arrived at the community hall, it was already half full, but we managed to get seats in the front row. A bunch of people carried signs that said SWIMMING POOL SUCKS and NO NEW TAXES. The chief business of the community council meeting was to discuss the proposal for a large indoor swimming pool for Partridge Cove.

Some people thought it would be a good recreational facility that would attract visitors and help the merchants and bed and breakfast operators. But others were against it because taxes would go up to pay for it. They thought the money should be spent on a park. Both sides had been arguing about it in the local paper for weeks.

My presentation was first on the agenda, and the chairperson waved at me to come up to the front. Then he banged on the table with a wooden hammer and called the meeting to order.

When he introduced me, somebody shouted, "What about the pool?" I looked at the chairperson, but he smiled and told me not to pay any attention and just go ahead.

At first my voice was really shaky, and one or two people shouted, "Can't hear," and "Tell her to speak up," so I began all over again.

"I think you all know the seniors' residence, Peacehaven," I said.

"Sure do. God's waiting room," a man at the back shouted, and a lot of people laughed.

When I told them about the plan to close Peacehaven and tear down the building, a man shouted, "Should have done it long ago." When I said it was a historic building that was worth saving, he shouted, "Why don't you get your old man to save it." Some people laughed, and others said, "Shut up, Charlie, give her a chance." The chairman said, "Order!" and told me to continue.

I said that if it was closed, members of the staff would lose their jobs. Then I said that the elderly residents thought of it as their home, and that a move at their time of life would upset them and could cause health problems.

Finally I told them about Mr. and Mrs. Renfrew who had been married for fifty years, and would be sent to separate homes for men and women, and wouldn't be able to live together ever again.

A hand at the back of the room shot up.

"I think somebody has a question for you, Ellen," the chairperson said. It was the rude man called Charlie. He stood up.

"There's an old saying. You don't know what happiness is till you get married, then it's too late," the man said. "If these Renfrews have been married for fifty years, I think they deserve a break. I know I would."

That got a big laugh, and someone shouted, "You and me both."

It was pretty embarrassing standing there while the whole room laughed. I could feel my face getting red and I didn't know if I was supposed to answer the question. I just wanted to sink through the floor.

When the laughing stopped, the chairperson asked if I had anything more to say. So I read the last paragraph, where I suggested ways to save Peacehaven, but I was so flustered by the laughing that I read too fast and stumbled over the words. My suggestions included circulating a petition to take to the government, and raising money for the new roof. I said that if we all worked together we could save our seniors' home and our heritage building. I hoped the council would form a steering committee right away.

"Yeah. Call it the Dead Brain Cell Committee," Charlie shouted.

The chairman thanked me for my presentation, and one or two people clapped and shouted, "Well done!" Nobody followed up on my suggestion to form a committee.

Then we all filed out of the front row and left. As we walked over to the car, I could hear the crowd inside still yelling.

"What do we want?"

"A pool!"

"When do we want it?"

"NOW!"

"Hi, hi, ho, ho! Swimming pool has gotta go!"

"How did it go?" said Mum when we got home.

"That was the worst display of bad manners I've come across in some time," Dad said.

"I'm never doing anything like that again," I said. "Everybody laughed at me."

"You should have let us heckle you when you were practicing," Toby said.

"Your face got bright red, Ellen," Tim said. "Even your ears got red."

"I think people in the country act much worse than they do in the city," Dimsie said. "There's a Crime Watch in my neighborhood in Toronto and our meetings are very polite and friendly."

"You mustn't judge everyone by that group," Dad said, when we were all sitting around the table and poking away at peaches and ice cream. "The worst people always make the most noise, so they seem more numerous than they really are. But it's entirely possible, Ellen, that your words had more effect than you think. My guess is that many people will feel ashamed tomorrow when they reflect that they were a party to such rudeness. So don't be too discouraged."

But the next day things didn't seem any better.

"Heard they gave you a hard time at the meeting last night," Mr. Banks said. He had a very annoying grin on his face.

"It was a bad time to make a presentation," Mrs. Banks said. "They're all riled up over this swimming pool business. Cathy said she'd been expecting trouble."

"It's much better to leave these matters to older people with more experience," Mrs. Fenwick said. "They are generally wiser in the ways of the world."

I thought they didn't seem very wise in the ways of the world to me.

16
FALL OUT

I'd almost forgotten about the community council meeting when Dad looked up from his paper one morning.

"Well, well, Ellen," he said. "It seems that your presentation to the community council didn't go unnoticed after all."

He folded back a page of the paper and handed it over to me. There was a long article under a big headline that said ANOTHER SENIORS' RESIDENCE THREATENED WITH CLOSURE.

An acrimonious meeting of the Partridge Cove Community Council over a proposed new swimming pool brought no resolution to the conflict.

The first item on the agenda was a proposal to oppose plans by the provincial government to close down a long-established seniors' home in the community and demolish the building.

Ellen Fremedon, a young volunteer at the facility, described the effect of job losses on the staff and the unfortunate effect that being moved to a larger facility would have on the long-term residents. Among those whose lives would be disrupted are Fred and Gladys Renfrew, a married couple who might have to go to separate facilities or be placed in separated living quarters for men and women.

I thought the write-up was pretty good, but the pictures were all mixed up and the captions underneath them were all wrong. There was a picture of Mr. and Mrs. Renfrew sitting side by side in their wheelchairs, holding hands. A caption underneath the picture said, "Together for fifty years now facing separation."

There was also a picture of Dimsie at Mrs. McCrorie's birthday party, and another one of her at the piano. The captions said "Dimsie Fairchild with her grandmother" and "Young volunteer tries to save Peacehaven." There was no picture of me, though I guess that was a good thing because I always look terrible in photographs.

There was a note at the bottom of the page.

This is the first of a series of articles on the remarkable residents of Peacehaven. Tomorrow: the storyteller and children's author, Josephine Gwillam, who writes under the name of Josie Williams.

"I didn't know Miss Gwillam was a writer," I said.

"I don't know Josephine Gwillam," Mum said, "but I certainly know the name Josie Williams. Don't you remember, Ellen, how you loved *The Lobster Who Thought the Fish Store Was a Pet Shop* when you were little? You made me read it to you until we both knew it by heart."

"I think I still have a copy," I said.

"Perhaps she'll autograph it for you. I think you should be very pleased with such excellent coverage, and I imagine the people at Peacehaven will be very grateful to you."

"Does it mean the government will change its mind about closing the place down?" I said.

"I wouldn't count on that," Dad said. "It takes more than a few articles in the paper to move the provincial government. And this isn't an election year. But you've certainly done your best and you should be proud of that."

But I was positive that newspaper readers would be mad about separating the Renfrews and shutting down Peacehaven. I couldn't wait to go out there to hear how the seniors felt about being written up in the paper.

When I walked into the lobby, the receptionist called out that Mrs. Fisher, the superintendent, wanted a word with me in the office.

"Ellen, I'm very exasperated by what you've done," Mrs. Fisher said, taking off her glasses and holding up a newspaper that was lying on her desk. "Going to the media is sure to annoy the minister of health. This will convince him to close Peacehaven."

"But he'd already decided to close it down," I said. "Only a few people knew about it. Now that everyone knows, a lot of people will write to the minister and tell him to keep it open."

"And where will that lead? It will lead to very ugly confrontations. It's much better to work behind the scenes diplomatically. You really should leave these things up to people with more experience. It's difficult enough to run a place like this, without having journalists on our backs. Now a grade school teacher wants to bring her class in to talk to Miss Gwillam. The staff can't have children running all over the place."

I was just about to say it wasn't fair to blame me, when the phone on the desk rang. Mrs. Fisher picked it up, her scowl changed to a smile, and she pointed towards the door. I tiptoed out and closed the door quietly, but not before I heard Mrs. Fisher say, "Good of you to call back, Minister. I'm sure this will all blow over."

I went down the hall to the Renfrews' room, where they were sitting side by side as usual. The paper was on the table with their cups and saucers.

"Ellen, I wish you'd warned me before your friend came to take our pictures," Mrs. Renfrew said. "I would have had my hair done. I look such a fright I'm quite embarrassed. I don't even want to send the picture to my daughter. She'd be shocked." Neither of them seemed particularly grateful.

Miss Gwillam wasn't too happy, either.

"Come in, Ellen," she said. "I want to tell you a story." I noticed a big FOR SALE sign on the mouse house, and I wondered if the mice were moving out, but her story was about something else.

"Once upon a time there was little girl who

loved to listen to a program for children on the wireless. She was a lonely child, and she listened every day. She felt that Daphne, her favorite story-teller on the program, was a personal friend. She had the most wonderful voice, light and gay. The little girl imagined how she looked — young and pretty, with long dark hair. Then one day she happened to see a picture of Daphne in the paper. What a shock! Daphne, the lady with the golden voice, was really a cross-looking old woman with spectacles on the end of her nose and gray hair done up in a bun. The little girl was so disappointed that she never listened to the program again. She felt betrayed.

"What does that tell you, Ellen?"

"The little girl shouldn't have judged the story-teller by how she looked," I said. "Some weird-looking people are very nice."

"I'm sure they are," Miss Gwillam said, "but that was not the point I wanted to make." She looked really annoyed.

"That little girl was me," she said. "And the story tells you why I avoid publicity. I don't have my picture on the jacket of my books, I avoid having my picture in the paper, and I don't want to meet my young readers. That's because I don't want to disappoint them. I want them to know me through my books. That way they can imagine an author who is young and attractive."

I thought that was pretty dumb but I didn't say so.

Mr. Martin was the only person who wasn't annoyed with me. He was chuckling when I went into his room.

"Well, it's a grand day for the race, isn't it, Ellen?" he said.

"What race?"

"The human race."

I'd never seen him so cheerful.

"I hear you've really put the cat among the pigeons, Ellen. All the old biddies are up in arms. Seems they've got their pictures in the paper, and they don't look like movie stars. Big surprise!"

"Did you get a letter from your son?" I said.

"Sure did. Got it this morning."

But Rupert Martin didn't say a word about the letter I'd sent him. He told his dad all about a trip he was taking to the high Arctic. He was going to Grise Bay where the landing strip was at the bottom of a sheer cliff, and then on over the mountains to Resolute Bay. He said it could be dangerous at this time of year but the pilots were very experienced and he was really excited.

"It's funny he doesn't say anything about closing

down Peacehaven," I said. "Do you think he got my letter?"

"Don't know," Mr. Martin said.

It was very frustrating. And Dimsie seemed to feel the same way.

"I'm not going out to Peacehaven tomorrow," she said. "I'm fed up with them. They didn't like Auld Lang Syne. They said it was too sad. All they want to hear is the Skye Boat Song and On the Bonnie Bonnie Banks of Loch Lomond. They want me to play the same old stuff over and over again so they can sing along. I've had it. Let's do something different tomorrow, go to the beach or something. You don't have to go out to Peacehaven every day, do you?"

"Well, I promised to get some tea for Miss Gwillam, and Mr. Martin wants to write a letter," I said. "But we can do something after I've done that. I'll come over as soon as I get back."

17
AN UNEXPECTED VISITOR

AFTER THE ARTICLE IN the paper there was a steady stream of visitors to Peacehaven. Some wandered around outside taking pictures of the building. Lots of people brought copies of Miss Gwillam's books for her to sign. The staff told them to wait on the veranda while they took the books in to her. Then they went away with the signed copies, disappointed that they didn't get to meet her.

"It's like Grand Central Station. All this traffic is making a lot of extra work for my staff, Ellen," Mrs. Fisher said, as if it was all my fault.

I was in Mr. Martin's room the next afternoon reading a letter from Rupert Martin about inukshuks, piles of rock that the Inuit set up to look like people. They used them to show the way to people traveling over the frozen tundra. Rupert had drawn a picture of one and it looked as if it would be pretty easy to make one. I thought I might set one up in our garden to point the way to Somecot.

Suddenly Mrs. Fisher appeared in the doorway looking even crankier than usual.

"We've got another visitor," she said. "This one wants to talk to you. I've told her to wait out on the veranda."

"Is she from a newspaper?" I said.

"I sincerely hope not," Mrs. Fisher said. "I don't think I can take much more of this."

The woman was sitting in a wicker chair and she didn't look like a reporter. Her hair was a mess, her clothes were rumpled, and she had bags under her eyes. When I said my name, she seemed disappointed.

"I came to see the girl who's trying to stop this place from being closed down," she said. Her hands were trembling.

"That's me."

"But you're not the girl whose picture was in the paper."

"No," I said. "They didn't take my picture because I'm not photogenic, with my glasses and all. They wanted someone pretty, so they took a picture of my friend instead, though all she does is play the piano for the seniors. I was the one who made a presentation at the council meeting, not Dimsie."

"Dimsie!?"

"It's Scottish," I said.

"Dimsie!" the woman said again. "She's your friend?"

"Yes," I said. "She doesn't live here, though. She's from Toronto. She's just out here for the summer."

"She's out here for the summer!" the woman repeated. She had a dazed look on her face, and I wondered if she had a touch of sun. She wasn't wearing a hat and the sun had been beating down all day.

"Would you like a glass of water?" I said, but she didn't answer.

"Her grandmother, the one in the picture with her… She's here, isn't she?"

"Oh, no. That wasn't her grandmother," I said. "The paper got every single thing wrong, as usual. That was Mrs. McCrorie. Dimsie's grandmother lives in the village."

"She lives in the village!"

"Yes," I said. "She's lived in Partridge Cove for about eight years. Dimsie's staying with her because her dad's spending the summer in Boston."

"In Boston!"

She repeated everything I said. Then she sat for a long time looking out over the lake, as if she had forgotten I was there.

By now she wasn't the only one who was trembling. I could feel my heart knocking against my rib cage because I was beginning to get this funny feeling.

I knew who she was. She wasn't as beautiful as the woman in the painting in the closet in Dimsie's room. She looked a lot older, and she didn't have long dark hair, but something about her face was the same.

"You're Catriona Broster, aren't you?" I said, and she looked at me as if she couldn't believe her ears.

"How do you know my name?"

"Well, Dimsie…" I was about to say she's been reading all your letters but I realized how funny that would sound.

"Does Dimsie speak of me?" she said.

"Oh, yes," I said. "She talks about you all the time."

"And my mother. Does she speak of me?"

"No."

Then, because her face seemed to crumple up, I thought I should try to explain.

"Maybe it would make her too sad, because she misses you."

There was another long silence.

"Did you hit your head on something?" I said.

"Hit my head? No, of course not. What an odd question! What did you say your name is?"

"Ellen Fremedon."

"Ah! Ellen Fremedon." She looked as if she didn't know what to do or say next.

"My gran always says there's nothing like a good strong cup of tea to…" I could hear the cups and saucers rattling inside for the afternoon tea. Then I had a second thought.

"Why don't you come to my house for tea? Do you have a car?"

"No car," she said. "I came over from the mainland on the ferry and took a taxi out here."

"I'll call my dad."

Mum answered the phone, and I quickly told her about Dimsie's mother. I said that she had come to Peacehaven, and she was ill. Dad drove out right away to pick us up, and when we got home Mum asked Catriona Broster if she'd had anything to eat. She said she wasn't hungry but she would like a cup of tea. When I handed her the tea, she picked up the cup with both hands, and held it the way you wrap your hands around a mug of hot chocolate when it's cold out. Then she blew on it for a while before she started to drink it thirstily.

The tea seemed to help. She definitely started to look better.

"Would you like a poached egg and some toast?" I said, because I sometimes make that for Mum when she's feeling weak. I didn't wait for an answer but went into the kitchen, popped some toast in the toaster and put two eggs in the poacher. Sometimes my poached eggs turn out too runny or too hard, but these turned out just right.

As she ate, it was clear that she was famished. So I made some more toast and set out a pot of marmalade. She ate that, too.

Soon she perked up the way a wilted flower perks up after you give it water. The four of us sat around the table, not saying much, but just drinking our tea and looking out over the garden. I guess we were all wondering what to say. I kept my fingers crossed that the twins wouldn't turn up any time soon.

"It would be strange just to land on the doorstep after all these years," Catriona said. "It would be a great shock for them. And besides, I must look like a fright."

"There's no hurry," Mum said. "You should rest a little first. Perhaps you would like to sleep for an hour or two."

"I couldn't possibly," Catriona said. "There are

too many things going round and round in my mind."

"Would it help to talk about them?" Mum said.

"I think it would. So much has happened to me that I don't understand it all myself. Perhaps if I tell you about it, it will help me to get things straight in my mind and make some sense of them. Besides," she said, smiling for the first time, "you've been so kind. I feel I owe you an explanation."

And so Dimsie's mother told us her story. It was very long and none of us spoke or moved until she had finished.

18
A SAD STORY

IT ALL BEGAN WITH a quarrel with my mother. I'd been offered a tour and I'd decided not to go. I wanted to stay at home with my baby daughter. My mother was angry because it was the chance of a lifetime, the kind of thing you can't turn down because you'd never be asked again. She kept telling me that opportunity only knocks once. I wondered if she was thinking of all the years of music lessons that would be wasted.

She was sitting beside me in the car, and my husband — who had no problem with my decision to abandon the tour — and my daughter were behind us, little Dimsie in her baby seat. I was so angry that I was driving too fast. My husband said, "Slow down, Cat, you'll get us all killed!"

That was the last thing I remembered when I woke up in a hospital bed. I didn't know where I was or how I'd got there. I looked at the person sleeping in the other bed, but she was a patient I didn't recognize. I thought I must get out of there immediately and go home to my daughter.

Then I heard voices at the nursing station outside my room.

"She was the driver and she was the only survivor," one nurse said.

"Poor thing! It would be better if she never woke up."

I sat there for a very long time, trying to absorb the fact that I was alone in the world without my daughter, without my family.

There were sandals under my bed, a coat hanging on a peg, a purse and some more clothes in the cupboard between the beds. It was late in the evening, the end of visiting hours, and the corridors were crowded with people leaving the hospital. I mingled with them. I walked outside and down the street, neither knowing nor caring where I was going.

Then I saw a large neon sign: BUS STATION. It seemed like an invitation. I wanted to go far, far away to a distant place where I knew no one, and no one knew me.

I went inside and there was an announcement that the bus to Vancouver was about to leave. I went to the ticket office, took money from the purse, bought a ticket and boarded the bus.

It was a very long journey. People got on and off along the way. Night followed day, and the passengers slept, the bus made stops at places where we could get off, stretch our legs and buy something to eat. One night as I slept, my purse disappeared. I was afraid to draw attention to myself by raising the alarm. But at the next stop I found a jeweler's shop, and I sold my rings. That gave me enough money for food for a few days.

Eventually I arrived in Vancouver early in the morning. I'd slept in my clothes for days, not combed my hair, and I looked like a homeless person, which in fact I was. Somehow I found my way to a shelter, where I was given a meal and a cot to sleep on.

The woman on the cot beside me was desperately ill and coughed all night. In the morning, two nuns from a nearby convent arrived. They examined the woman and agreed to take her into their hospice.

"Take me, too, and I'll look after her," I said.

They assumed that I was the poor soul's friend or relative and allowed me to go along. I stayed with the woman, looking after her until she coughed for the last time. By then I'd made myself so useful that nobody wanted me to leave. The hospice was a clean and quiet place where the sick and elderly were well cared for. It became a refuge for me, and I felt that by looking after others I was atoning for the terrible thing I had done.

The sisters had a habit of taking in refugees and asking few questions. They had turned their backs on the world and understood my need for solitude and silence. I asked only for a bed and my meals, and to be allowed to care for the old and ailing patients. So they let me stay. I don't think they realized at the beginning how long that would be. Perhaps I would have stayed there for the rest of my life if it hadn't been for the picture in the paper.

I rarely read the papers, but one day an elderly patient was sitting in a chair while I made her bed. One of her visitors had left a newspaper.

"It's shameful," she said to me, "this closing down of homes, and old people with nowhere to go. Here's this one poor soul being driven out of the place that's been her home for years. Perhaps Sister Marguerite could bring her here." Then she showed me the picture.

I looked at the picture of the woman and the girl standing beside her. Of course, the pictures meant

nothing but the girl's name jumped out at me:
DIMSIE.

There could be only one Dimsie. It was such an
unusual name, the name of my husband's great-
aunt in Scotland. Then I saw the second name —
Fairchild. Then I saw the picture. It was of a girl the
exact age my daughter would be if there had been
no car accident.

I couldn't stop looking at the picture of my
daughter and the person I thought was my mother
— aged beyond belief.

While I looked, I kept hearing again in my head
the conversations of that long-ago day. "She was
driving and she was the only one who survived.
Poor thing, it would be better if she never woke up."

I remembered the patient sleeping her drugged
sleep in the next bed. The one whose purse I had
taken.

Was it possible my daughter and my husband
and my mother had been at home and safe all the
time?

"That's the saddest story I ever heard," I said.

"It is a sad story," Mum said, "but I believe it will
have a happy ending."

"I think I am ready for the ending," Catriona
said.

"I think you are, too," Mum said, "because you've had days to think about the outcome. Your family will be overjoyed, but initially it will be a shock."

"It won't be a total shock for Dimsie," I said, "because she's read your letters and read the newspaper clippings about you. She said she feels like she knows you."

"I think perhaps, if you will allow me, I should go over there ahead of you and prepare them for your arrival," Dad said.

"I'll go, too," I said.

"I think it would be better if you stayed here," Mum said.

"That's not fair…"

"You stay here, Ellen," Dad said.

It made me mad that I was the one who'd met Catriona and brought her home, and yet I wasn't allowed to tell Dimsie I'd found her.

It seemed ages before Dad came back and told Catriona that her mother and daughter were waiting to meet her. He'd left the car running on the driveway.

"I think I'd like to walk there, if it isn't too far," Catriona said.

"I'll show you the way," I said.

Mum and Dad frowned, but Catriona said she'd like me to go with her, so they didn't manage to leave me out after all.

We set off together for The Meads.

19
A REUNION

CATRIONA WALKED UP THE road very slowly. I couldn't tell if she was tired or just nervous.

"Goodness, what a dark and gloomy place," she said when we reached the gate at the end of the driveway. About halfway up she took my hand and squeezed it. She squeezed so hard it hurt, but I don't think she realized she was doing it.

When we finally rounded the last bend, I could see that the front door was open, and Mrs. Broster and Dimsie were waiting by the doorway.

Mrs. Broster stepped out when she saw us, and Catriona dropped my hand and went slowly towards her. They stared at each other for quite a while, and then hugged each other and stood back again and looked at each other.

"You've changed," Mrs. Broster said.

"You, too," Catriona said.

They didn't seem to know what to do next, and then Catriona spotted Dimsie standing behind Mrs. Broster.

"So this is Dimsie," she said. "Just like the picture in the paper. You were a baby when last I saw you."

Dimsie just stared at her mother and didn't say anything.

It wasn't at all like I'd expected. I thought they'd run toward each other, shouting and crying the way people do on TV when they've won something.

"Well, why are we all standing here?" Mrs. Broster said. And she turned around and went inside the house. Catriona followed slowly and then Dimsie.

"What a big house," Catriona said as she stood in the hallway, looking at the staircase.

"Can I take your coat?" Mrs. Broster said.

"I don't have a coat," Catriona said.

"Oh, yes, quite."

It was terrible. I thought if they carried on like that, Catriona was going to turn around and head straight back to Vancouver.

Maybe Dimsie was thinking the same thing, because she looked as if she was going to cry.

"Would anyone like a cup of tea?" I said suddenly.

They all three looked at me at once and said yes.

"The kitchen's through here," Mrs. Broster said, and she sort of pushed Catriona through a doorway and they sat around the kitchen table.

I was so nervous making tea while they all watched me without saying a word that I got everything mixed up. Maybe I was thinking of Gran's one spoonful for each person and one for the pot, because I put four tea bags in the pot. Then I took the kettle off the burner before the water was boiling properly.

But at least the rattle of cups and saucers broke that terrible silence. I poured the tea and even without letting it steep I could see it was way too strong.

Catriona picked up her cup with both hands as if she wanted to warm them, just as she'd done at our house. Then she leaned forward and blew on the tea.

Suddenly Mrs. Broster burst out laughing.

"Cat," she said, "you haven't changed a bit! For heaven's sakes, you still hold your cup like that, and blow on your tea. It used to drive me crazy."

Catriona looked startled, and then she started to laugh, too.

"It used to drive me crazy when you nagged me about it," she said. And they both laughed and laughed.

"Well, it's wonderful to see you blowing on your tea again," Mrs. Broster said.

Then they got up and hugged each other, and I couldn't tell whether they were laughing or crying. Dimsie and I just looked at each other. Finally they calmed down.

"I always knew we'd find you again," Mrs. Broster said.

"You did?" Catriona said.

"I never stopped searching for you. And I kept your piano…"

"You did? Ellen told me you never listen to music."

"After you first disappeared, I couldn't bear to hear music. It carried too many memories. I simply shut it out of my life altogether. But I kept your piano tuned. I couldn't even stay in the house while it was being tuned."

"That was why you went down to the city that day!" I said, but they completely ignored me.

"I wanted the piano to be ready so that when you came back, you could just sit down and play again. It would be as if you never went away."

"Where is it?" Catriona said.

Mrs. Broster took a key out of one of the kitchen drawers and went across the hall to a closed door. We all trailed after her. She opened it with a key, and we followed her inside. Then she stepped across the room and pulled at a big sheet covering a large piece of furniture. Underneath it was a very large piano.

"My old Steinway," Catriona said. She moved across the room, sat on the piano bench, opened the piano, stroked it and put her hands on the keys. Then she stopped.

"I haven't played for so long," she said. "I'm far too rusty."

"Do you want me to play?" Dimsie said. And she walked over to the piano and played her Chopin recital piece. It sounded even better than it did on the piano at Peacehaven.

When she'd finished, she looked around. Her mother was sitting on the couch with her head in her hands.

"Did I make too many mistakes?" Dimsie said, looking at her anxiously.

"No, no. It was beautiful," her mother said. "It was the most beautiful thing I ever heard in my life."

"I never knew she could play like that," Mrs. Broster said.

"You never knew?" Catriona said. "Didn't you ever hear her?"

I could see they all had a lot of explaining to do, and it was beginning to get to me. I stood up and was just about to say that I'd better be getting home, when I realized nobody would notice whether I was there or not. So I just got up and slipped out of the room.

I thought of going into the kitchen and throwing out that terrible tea and washing up the cups, but then I looked at the front door. It was still open because nobody had bothered to close it, and my feet just carried me outside. I closed the door quietly behind me.

I took a big breath of fresh air. Then I went down the driveway slowly, enjoying the smell of the laurels and the pine trees.

When I got home, I went straight down to Somecot and sat on the steps, feeling very confused.

I wished I hadn't gone. Maybe I was just too nosy, always snooping around, listening to other people's conversations and poking my nose into things that were none of my business.

I started thinking about mothers and daughters. Catriona and Dimsie both played the piano and liked the same kind of music. Anne and Jenny both liked decorating rooms and making things pretty. Then I got to wondering about the mother who had put me up for adoption, and if we would be alike, too.

The only person I want to talk to when I get down on myself like this is Jenny. I wished she hadn't gone away for the summer because I really, really missed her just then.

20
AN INVITATION

THE NEXT MORNING AT breakfast I said I wondered if I'd ever hear from Dimsie again.

"I wouldn't count on seeing her for a few days," Dad said. "It will take some time for those three women to get used to the new situation, and to catch up on the past ten years and make arrangements for the future."

"Maybe Dimsie and her mum will just go back to Toronto without even saying goodbye," Timmy said.

I felt even more let down at Peacehaven because everyone kept asking about Dimsie.

"Where's your pretty friend?"

"Where's your talented friend? When is she coming back to play the piano for us?"

"Her mother's turned up," I said. "I guess they're going shopping and doing stuff together."

Only Mr. Martin didn't ask about Dimsie. He had a letter from his son and I read it to him. It was about the Inuit hunting for polar bears and seals. They use every bit of the animal they hunt. They eat the meat. They use the skins to make coats and moccasins, and they even use the bones to make tools and carvings.

In the old days, they carved animals as charms to bring them luck and protect them when they went hunting. Now they sell carvings to make money to live on. If you go to a restaurant in the Arctic they come around while you're eating to show you their carvings and you can buy them. Mr. Martin said Rupert had sent him some carvings and he'd show them to me next time I went out there.

"Dimsie phoned right after you left this morning," Tim said as we were finishing lunch.

"And she called twice after that," Toby said.

"She called three times and nobody told me?"

"Forgot," Tim said.

"You must have amnesia or Alzheimer's or something," I said.

"Oh, Ellen," Dimsie said when I called, "I've been dying to talk to you. I wanted you to come over for lunch but you didn't call back."

"I only just got the message."

"Well, can you come and eat with us tonight? We're going to make a special supper. We have tons of things to show you."

"Will you be leaving soon?"

"No, but my mother will. That's why we want you to come over tonight. She's going to take a float-plane over to the mainland tomorrow to meet my dad. He's coming up from Boston. Granny says they'll need to be alone for a while. But when I go back to Toronto at the end of the summer we'll be a family. I'll tell you everything when I see you."

It really seemed strange going to the front door instead of climbing in the window. The house looked so different. The curtains were all open, and there was no light coming from Dimsie's window. I sort of missed the gloomy way it used to look. I felt left out, as if they all had each other and wouldn't want me around.

"I was looking out the window for you," Dimsie said when she opened the door.

Then she took me on a tour of the house. All the upstairs rooms were open. The sheets had been taken off the furniture and the rooms were bright and full of flowers. There were huge pianos in two of the rooms.

"This one's my mother's piano," Dimsie said.

"There were two grand pianos in the house the whole time that I could have been practicing on."

Then we went to the kitchen, where Mrs. Broster and Dimsie's mother were cooking. Mrs. Broster looked so different. Instead of the usual black, she was wearing a green dress with bright yellow flowers on it.

She took a roast chicken out of the oven.

"I hope you'll like this, Ellen," she said. "And we've got an ice-cream dessert because Dimsie says it's your favorite."

While we were having supper, I started to feel better about everything. Mrs. Broster wasn't going to move back east.

"I've got used to a quiet place," she said, "though it won't be as quiet as it was because Cat and Dimsie will be out here fairly often."

"Will you come out every summer?" I said.

"I'm sure we will," Catriona said. "And we'll be out for Christmas as well. But, Ellen, you must come to Toronto and visit us, too. We must definitely plan that. You're almost a member of the family now."

The supper was unbelievable, especially the dessert. Mrs. Broster put a kind of igloo of ice cream on a board, and she scooped beaten-up egg whites all over it and popped it in the oven. She explained that you have to do this really quickly so that the meringue cooks but the ice cream doesn't melt. It was called Baked Alaska. There was a chocolate sauce to pour over it, and you could put as much of it on as you wanted. I couldn't wait to tell the twins about it.

After dessert, all three of them played the piano. Dimsie's mum and grandmother said they played badly because they were so out of practice, but I didn't notice. Dimsie played the Chopin pieces that were her favorites, and we all clapped. Catriona said she couldn't believe her daughter was such a good pianist, and soon they would play duets together.

"Is it really hard to play Chopin?" I said.

"Would you like to learn how to play the piano?" Mrs. Broster asked. "You could be my first student."

"I don't have a piano," I said. "And don't lessons cost a lot of money?"

"I'm out of practice as a teacher, so we could learn together. I'd like to do something to repay you for all you've done for us. We're so grateful to you, Ellen. If it hadn't been for your work to save Peacehaven…"

"I'd like to take lessons," I said, "but I don't think I'd be very good. I'm no good at singing, and nobody in my family is very musical."

"Something tells me you have a good ear," Mrs. Broster said. "It's clear that you appreciate music, and that's an important first step. As for not having an instrument to practice on, you can easily come over here."

All three of them smiled at me in such an encouraging way that I got a fluttery feeling in my stomach.

Everybody I knew was good at something. Jenny could draw, Dimsie could play the piano and even Peggy Floyd got ribbons for riding her horse. People said they were gifted. Well, maybe I could have a gift, too. Even if it was just a small one, I thought I could make it bigger if I worked really hard at it.

"Can I start right away?" I said.

21
MORE SURPRISES

IT MIGHT SOUND LIKE we'd had enough surprises for one summer, but there were more to come. The next one happened when I went to Peacehaven with a bunch of sweetpeas and some diabetic shortbread cookies for Mr. Martin.

His door was wide open. There was no sign of Mr. Martin or his wheelchair, and Kelly was cleaning out the room.

She said he'd been taken by ambulance to the hospital in the city.

I suddenly felt very cold, and when I spoke, my voice sounded far away.

"Where did he go?"

Kelly said I'd better go and talk to Mrs. Fisher.

"Oh, there you are, Ellen," Mrs. Fisher said. "I

was hoping you'd stop by. Sit down, dear." She was so friendly that I was very suspicious. I didn't sit down.

"Mr. Martin's not coming back, is he?" I said.

"No, he isn't. He needs more care than we can give him."

"But he likes it here. All the noise in the city will make him sick."

"Ellen, Mr. Martin isn't concerned about noise at the moment. He's in the intensive care unit."

"Did you tell his son?" I said.

"Please sit down," she said again. So I did. I was still holding the sweetpeas and the cookies.

"Ellen," she said, "Mr. Martin's son died some years ago in a plane crash in the high Arctic."

"No, he didn't. He wrote letters to Mr. Martin all the time. I read them to him."

"Ellen, the letters you read were written years ago. They were quite old."

"But Mr. Martin wrote back. I helped him."

"I know you did, Ellen. The letters were never sent because there was no one to send them to. I have them here in my desk."

She pulled a bunch of letters out of a drawer and set them on the desk. They were all the letters I'd written.

"You mean I was spending my time writing letters that never got sent?" I said. "I don't get it. Did Mr. Martin have amnesia or something? Did he think his son was still alive?"

"I believe he wanted to think so, and the letters he dictated to you helped him to believe it. They were a way of keeping his son's memory alive. And he was very grateful that you helped him to do that."

"Well, you'd never know it."

"Some people find it hard to express their thanks in words. However, he left you something."

There was a big square box on the table. She brought it over and put it on the desk in front of me.

I could see that someone had printed something on the lid in a very shaky hand:

for my little friend Ellin Fremdon xox

I lifted the lid off the box and saw our tea cozy, the earmuffs I'd lent Mr. Martin, and the slippers that Dad was still looking for.

Underneath there was a package of letters from Mr. Martin's son — a lot more than the ones I had read. They were in their envelopes, and I could see from the postmarks and stamps that they had been written over many years. I lifted them out and got down to the bottom layer of box.

It was filled with carvings so tiny that each one was about as big as my thumb. There was a bear with a fish in its mouth, a bear that was dancing with its leg up, a seal lying on its back, and an inukshuk. They were all carved out of gray stone speckled with white.

I set them in a row on the desk. There was one more carving that was bigger than the others. It was a person on a sled and a lot of dogs pulling the sled, all of them attached to each other with thread. They were carved out of white bone. I lifted these out carefully and put them beside the stone ones.

Mrs. Fisher got up and came around to look at them from the front. Just then Kelly popped her head in the door, and Mrs. Fisher told her to come in, too.

"I don't think you can say now that Mr. Martin didn't appreciate your help," Mrs. Fisher said.

"Lord, no, he never stopped asking when Ellen was coming in," Kelly said. "Used to drive me crazy. You could get a fortune for those carvings, if you ever decided to sell them."

"Well, I won't," I said. "I'll keep them forever to remind me of Mr. Martin. And I'll write him a long letter. Do you think the nurses will have time to read it to him?"

"I'm sure they will," Mrs. Fisher said.

I was wondering how I'd get everything home on my bike, when Kelly said she'd give me a ride if I didn't mind waiting until the end of her shift. So I went in to visit with Miss Gwillam until she was ready.

"Come in and sit down, Ellen," Miss Gwillam said, "and I'll tell you about Jasmine's latest escapade."

I sat in the window seat looking at the lake, hoping it wouldn't be a very long story. After a while, though, I got interested. It's always like that with Miss Gwillam. It's the way she tells it.

"Jasmine Mousefield had taken out a library book called *Whiskerella*. It was about a poor little mouse and her mean stepsisters. Jasmine loved it and carried the book wherever she went. Now you know how thoughtless Jasmine can be."

"Yes," I said. "She wouldn't even share her Christmas chocolates with the others."

"Well, she lost the book. That made her very sad. She didn't give a thought to other mice who might want to read it. She simply worried that she'd never know what happened after the prince put the glass slipper on Whiskerella's hind paw. She asked each sister in turn how it ended, but none of them would tell her.

"A few days later Jasmine found the book in the garden. It had been out in the rain all night and the print had washed off the pages. When she returned it, the librarian gave her a fine and a scolding. Two big tears trickled down her nose and ran along her whiskers. But do you suppose she was ashamed of herself?"

"Yes," I said.

"Well, you suppose wrong," Miss Gwillam said. "She was in despair because she'd never know what happened to Whiskerella. But just then a more responsible mouse returned a copy of the same book. Jasmine grabbed it, sat down and read the ending. She was so pleased to learn that Whiskerella and the Prince lived happily ever after that she vowed never to treat a book carelessly ever again."

Miss Gwillam waited for me to say something, as she always did at the end of a story.

"What will you do when Peacehaven closes down?" I said.

"Oh, dear me!" she said. "There'll be a great upheaval and turmoil. But eventually the dust will settle. I don't suppose the Mousefields or I will ever be the same again. But change is not something to fear, Ellen. There will be new stories to tell."

Just then I heard Kelly calling me.

"Goodbye, Miss Gwillam," I said.

"Goodbye, Ellen Fremedon. Don't worry about the mice and me. We shall be just fine."

"Kelly," I said, as she was driving me home, "did you know the letters from Mr. Martin's son were old ones?"

"Sure," Kelly said. "He was always getting them out and wanting me to read them to him, but I just couldn't get interested in reading a lot of old letters from someone who died a long time ago."

"And when I gave you the letters to mail to his son, didn't you think that was weird?"

"Look, Ellen, you work at a place like this long enough, you see a lot of crazy stuff. I don't let it faze me, and I never ask people why they do what they do. I figure they have their reasons. From what I read in the paper, the people out there running things in the world are a lot crazier than the folks at Peacehaven. That's the scary part."

"What will you do when Peacehaven closes down?" I said.

"Get me another job, I guess."

"In the city?"

"Lord, I hope not. I live with my mum and she'll never move. But I might have to. There isn't a whole lot of work around Partridge Cove these days."

When we got home, Kelly helped me with my

bike, and I carried the shoe box into the house very carefully.

"Come in and meet my dad," I said. What Kelly said about never questioning why people do the things they do had given me an idea.

Dad was at the kitchen sink peeling carrots.

"Dad," I said, "this is Kelly. She works at Peace-haven."

"Hello, Kelly. Nice to meet you," he said.

"She won't have a job after Peacehaven closes down, and she doesn't want to work in the city."

"Can't say I blame her."

"Dad," I said, "Kelly says it doesn't faze her when people do a lot of crazy things. She never questions why they do the things they do. And she likes look-ing after people."

"Is that so?" Dad said. He put the carrots in a bowl, rinsed off his hands, dried them on a tea towel and came out of the kitchen.

"Perhaps Kelly and I should have a little chat," he said.

When they came out of his study, they were both smiling, and he walked Kelly out to her truck and shook hands with her. At supper he told us Kelly was going to start working for us as soon as Peacehaven closed down.

"So all the time you spent at Peacehaven brought some good results," Mum said.

It was true. I hadn't managed to stop Peacehaven from closing down, but I'd made new friends, and I was going to start taking piano lessons. And it would be great to have a housekeeper again.

The only thing was, I didn't think Kelly would have much chance of meeting Mr. Right while she was working for us.

22
THE SUMMER READING PROGRAM

DIMSIE AND I SPENT every day together before she left. She practised the piano while I listened. She taught me to play "Twinkle Twinkle, Little Star," which sounded stupid at first. Then we played it as a duet and it sounded great. I started my own lessons with Mrs. Broster, mostly learning little kid songs, but I didn't mind. That still left us plenty of time to go out to Peacehaven, ride our bikes, have picnics, pick blackberries, walk on the beach, and just sit and talk.

I don't know if it was finding her mother or finding her piano that changed Dimsie the most, but she sure was different. She stopped saying Partridge Cove was a boring dump.

"Do you still cross off the days on your calendar to make the summer go quickly?" I said.

"I do cross the days off," she said, "but now I feel bad when I see I have only a few days left."

She was looking forward to having a regular family with a mum and dad in Toronto, but she said she was going to miss Granny Broster and me. She thought Partridge Cove was the best place in the world to spend holidays. We made a lot of plans for when she came back next summer. And we promised to write every week.

The day after she left, I went down to the library. I was looking for a book about the Arctic, but Miss Jane Green was on the desk, and I knew she would tell me to go to the computer to look it up. It was easier just to ask Larry, but he was reading to the kids in the summer reading program.

I could hear his voice coming from the children's section, so I went over there and leaned against the bookcase to wait until he finished.

He was squeezed into one of the little kid chairs with a pile of books on the table beside him. About ten kids were in the room. One was sitting on a bean bag chair and picking the stitches out of it. The others were lying around the floor, sucking their thumbs or picking their noses, and some were hugging stuffed animals. They were all squirming around like worms when you dig a spade into the ground. No one was listening, and one kid was pinching the arm of the boy next to him. Their parents had probably dumped them there while they went shopping.

"...he found his supper waiting for him and it was still hot," Larry read in a bored voice. Then he closed the book and picked up another one.

"Mousefield Park is a large house in the country," he read. "It is the home of a family of field mice. Their names are Jessie, Jemima, Japonica, Josephine and Jasmine..." He stumbled over the names, and he didn't pronounce Jasmine properly.

"Larry," I said. "Do you want me to read that?"

Larry looked up in surprise, and all the little kids turned around and stared at me.

"Sure," he said. "Plenty of other stuff I could be doing."

So I took his place on the little chair and picked up the book.

"It is the home of a family of field mice," I read, "and their names are Jessie, Jemima, Japonica, Josephine and Jasmine..."

I paused after each name just the way Miss Gwillam did when she talked about the mice. When I got to the part about the last present that was left under the Christmas tree, I stopped alto-gether.

"Do you know who it was from?" I said, and I looked around at each of the kids. The one on the bean bag chair took his thumb out of his mouth and said, "Uh-uh," and the others shook their heads.

"It was from Jasmine to *herself*," I said in exact-ly the same disapproving tone that Miss Gwillam used. All the time I was reading, I seemed to hear Miss Gwillam's voice like an echo in my head. The kids all stopped squirming, and when I finished they were as quiet as mice themselves. One had fallen fast asleep.

I looked at them the way Miss Gwillam did when she finished a story.

"What did you think of that?" I said.

"I liked it," one said.

"Read it again," the kid on the bean bag chair said.

Then I saw that Miss Jane Green was standing by the bookcases listening as well.

"How well you read that, Ellen!" she said. "I've never known the children to be so attentive. You have a real gift."

"Do you think you could come in and read again, Ellen?" Larry said. "There's another week in the reading program, and we're pretty busy just now with all the summer visitors returning their books. I could waive your fines."

"Sure," I said.

"Now that Dimsie's left, and you aren't spending quite so much time out at Peacehaven," Mum said at lunch, "do you think you could do something in the garden tomorrow? The cottage garden's full of weeds."

"Well, I've got a piano lesson," I said. "Plus I promised Larry I'd read to the kids in the summer reading program."

"Oh, really? I thought you refused when he asked you at the beginning of the summer."

"I did, but I've changed my mind."

I started thinking about everything that had happened in the past two months. I'd made a billion cups of tea and I'd listened to a billion stories — Rupert Martin's stories of the Arctic, Mrs. Renfrew's stories of Korea, Miss Gwillam's ones about the mice, and Catriona Broster's story of her life. There were so many different kinds of stories. Some were happy and some were sad. Some were real people and some were imaginary, but all of them were true in a way.

And all the stories I'd heard ran like streams

flowing into one big pond, and that pond was my own story of the summer.

If I told my own story, I wondered what kind of a story it would be. I knew it would be quite long and complicated, with lots of chapters.

23
JENNY'S RETURN

I WAS SITTING AT my desk in Somecot writing a letter to Dimsie. I had a lot to tell her.

Dear Dimsie,
This is what I did last week. I rode out to Peacehaven. Miss Gwillam has a new hat that looks like an upside-down plant pot.

Gran came for lunch on Sunday and sends her regards. Tim says you should wear a mask because the air in the city is polluted and can give you asthma. He left the medical diction-ary on the beach, and the tide came in and swept it out to sea, so his medical career's on hold. The twins bought a goldfish bowl in a garage sale. They are giving it to Gran with

*two goldfish for her birthday. I got a dish in
the same sale. I'm making Gran a garden in
the bowl with cactus and succulent plants
and a little gravel path.*

I was just going to tell her that I'd had two piano lessons and practiced a lot of scales, when I was interrupted by a familiar voice calling my name.

"Ellen, Ellen, I'm home!"

It was Jenny.

I'd forgotten all about Jenny coming home, and suddenly there she was standing in the doorway of Somecot with a gift-wrapped package in her hand and a big smile on her face.

I was so surprised I didn't move.

"Aren't you glad to see me?" Jenny said, her smile fading away.

"Of course," I said. "I'm surprised, though. I didn't expect you so soon."

"Well, I was supposed to stay with Dad and Sally in Vancouver, but they were going away for the weekend so I came straight on home."

"Oh."

"Did you miss me?"

"I guess so, but I was pretty busy."

"With gardening?"

"I didn't do much gardening. I did some volunteer work at Peacehaven and I read to the kids in the summer reading program, and I spent a lot of time with Dimsie."

"I thought you hated reading to kids. And who's Dimsie? What kind of a dumb name is that?"

"It's a Scottish name and she's a girl from Toronto. Mrs. Broster's granddaughter."

"Is she the one who borrowed my bike without asking and left it with a flat tire?"

"Anne said it was okay. You weren't here to ask."

"You could have written and told me. You didn't write once."

"I started to," I said. "Anyway, you didn't write me any letters."

"I sent postcards every week. Didn't you get them?"

"Yes. Thanks."

"What are you doing?"

"Writing a letter."

"Who to?"

"To Dimsie. She wrote me this letter," I said, handing Dimsie's letter over to Jenny. "It's written in code. You only read every third word — "

"A secret code? It sounds like something the twins would do. Is she the same age as the twins?"

"No, she's our age. She's fun."

"Sounds like you made a new friend while I

was away and you like her better than me," Jenny said.

"You don't have to get mad," I said. "A person can have two friends, can't she?"

"Forget it!" Jenny said. She started to leave and then turned back.

"Oh, I brought you a present," she said. Then she threw the package on my desk.

After she left, I opened it. There were two white T-shirts inside. One had a picture of the skyline of a city and the words REGINA THE QUEEN CITY on it, and the other had a picture of a grain elevator and the words SASKATCHEWAN BREAD BASKET OF THE WORLD.

"Did I hear Jenny's voice just now?" Mum said at lunch. "I thought Anne said she wasn't coming back until next week."

"She came home early," I said. "I don't think Jenny and I are going to be friends anymore."

"Why, whatever happened?" Mum said, looking at me in surprise.

"I didn't act all happy to see her because I wasn't expecting her, and I was writing a letter to Dimsie and so she thinks Dimsie is my best friend now. She brought me back two T-shirts, too," I said. "I should have given her a welcome home present, I guess."

"It's not too late."

"I don't know what to give her. I'm no good at thinking up presents."

"What about the miniature garden you were making for Gran?" Mum said. "You have time to make another one for Gran's birthday."

"I don't have another bowl."

"Well, you can easily find something else. What about a wicker basket? They're fairly cheap. You could make a herb garden or something. Gran would like that."

So, after lunch, I got busy putting the finishing touches on the garden. I had a miniature palm tree, a cactus and some hen-and-chicks succulent plants along a little gravel path, and I put a tiny seat from an old doll's house under the tree.

Then I made a card with a picture of an inuk-shuk.

I carried the bowl over to Jenny's house.

When I rang the bell, Jenny opened the door.

"I made this for you," I said.

"Oh, what a beautiful bowl," Jenny said. "It's gorgeous!"

"I should have gift-wrapped it, but I didn't have time to buy wrapping paper."

"So that's why you looked so stunned when I turned up," Jenny said. "You were working on a surprise and you didn't have it ready."

"Right," I said, looking down at my sneakers.

"And all I gave you were two lousy T-shirts that I bought on sale at the Regina airport."

"I really like them," I said. "I didn't make much money this summer and I need new clothes for school."

So we went into Jenny's room and Jenny put the miniature garden on her desk. Then she showed me the portfolio of work she'd done at the art school and I told her about my Inuit carvings.

Soon we were thinking what a short time we had before school started, and how we should get busy rounding up school supplies. Jenny said we should get together the next morning and make a list of all the stuff we needed.

"What did you get with your book certificate?" she said.

"I haven't cashed it in yet."

"You haven't cashed it in?"

"I didn't get around to it. You can help me pick something out."

It takes a while to get used to people again when you've been separated for two months. But soon we were back to our normal selves, and it was as if Jenny had never gone away.

Even though we quarrel and argue, and even though I make new friends, she will always be my best friend.

JOAN GIVNER, a former university English professor, is a writer and book reviewer who has written a dozen books of biography, autobiography and fiction, including *Katherine Anne Porter: A Life* and the novels *Half Known Lives* and *Playing Sarah Bernhardt.* She has written two previous books about Ellen Fremedon — *Ellen Fremedon* (nominated for the Silver Birch and Hackmatack awards) and *Ellen Fremedon, Journalist* (nominated for the Diamond Willow Award). She lives on Vancouver Island in Mill Bay, a small seaside town not unlike Partridge Cove.